Divine Cozy Mystery ~~~~   **3**

Hope Callaghan

hopecallaghan.com

Visit my website for new releases and special offers: hopecallaghan.com

Thank you to these wonderful ladies who help make my books shine - Peggy H., Cindi G., Jean P., Wanda D., Barbara W. and Renate P. for taking the time to preview *Divine Blindside,* for the extra sets of eyes and for catching all of my mistakes.

i

Acknowledgments

A special THANKS to my reader review team:

Alice, Alta, Amary, Becky, Brinda, Carolyn, Cassie, Charlene, Christina, Debbie, Denota, Devan, Diann, Grace, Jan, Jo-Ann, Joyce, Jean K., Jean M., Judith, Katherine, Lynne, Megan, Melda, Kat, Linda, Lynne, Pat, Patsy, Paula, Rebecca, Rita, Tamara, Theresa, Valerie, Vicki and Virginia.

CONTENTS

Cast of Characters

Joanna "Jo" Pepperdine. After suffering a series of heartbreaking events, Jo Pepperdine decides to open a halfway house, for recently released female convicts, just outside the small town of Divine, Kansas. She assembles a small team of new friends and employees to make her dream a reality. Along the way, Jo comes to realize that not only has she given some women a new chance at life, she's given herself a new lease on life, too.

Delta Childress. Delta is Jo's second in command. She and Jo become fast friends after Jo hires her to run the bakery and household. Delta is a no-nonsense asset, with a soft spot for the women who arrive broken, homeless, hopeless and needing a hand up. Although Delta isn't keen on becoming involved in the never ending string of mysteries around town, she finds herself in over her head more often than not.

Raylene Baxter. Raylene is among the first women to come to the farm, after being released from *Central State Women's Penitentiary*. Raylene, a former bond agent / bounty hunter, has a knack for sleuthing out clues and helping Jo catch the bad guys.

iv

Nash Greyson. Nash, Jo's right-hand man, is the calming force in her world of crisis. He's opposed to Jo and Delta sticking their nose into matters that are better left to the law, but often finds himself right in the thick of things, rescuing Delta and Jo when circumstances careen out of control.

Gary Stein. Gary, a retired farmer, works his magic in Jo's gardens. A widower, he finds purpose helping Jo and the farm. Gary catches Delta's eye and Jo has to wonder if there isn't a second chance...at love for Gary and Delta, too.

"Brothers and sisters, I do not consider myself yet to have taken hold of it. But one thing I do: Forgetting what is behind and straining toward what is ahead..." Philippians 3:13 (NIV)

Chapter 1

"I hope you have a wonderful day at work and rake in a ton of tips." Joanna Pepperdine gave Sherry an encouraging smile.

"Thanks, Jo. Me, too." Sherry gave Jo a thumbs up and hopped out of the SUV. "My shift ends at one o'clock, right after the lunch hour rush."

"I'll be here to pick you up then. See you later." She watched Sherry step into the *Divine Delicatessen* and offered up a small prayer.

Jo's friend, Marlee Davison, the owner of *Divine Delicatessen*, had recently hired Sherry Marshall, one of Jo's residents and a former female convict at the local prison, to work part-time in the nearby town of Divine.

She was the first to approach Marlee about hiring one of her residents. The timing was perfect since her friend claimed she was getting ready to add wait staff for the fall season.

She knew exactly which woman would be a perfect fit for the position...Sherry, and although any of the women would have been a good candidate, Sherry was the first one who came to mind. She was the one Jo deemed most in need of building some self-confidence.

Jo was halfway home before she realized Sherry had forgotten her backpack with her work uniform inside. She returned to the deli and found Sherry inside standing next to another woman, an employee.

"What do you mean you don't have your uniform?" The older woman shoved a hand on her hip. "If you don't have a uniform, you don't work. Marlee will send you home."

"Please..." Sherry reached for the woman's arm. "It's in the SUV. I'm sure Jo will bring it to me."

"This is ridiculous," the woman snapped.

Neither woman noticed Jo approach. "Hey, Sherry. I realized your backpack was on the front seat."

"Thanks, Jo. I was getting ready to call you. I'll go change." Sherry grabbed the backpack and darted down the hallway leaving Jo and the scowling woman alone.

"I don't believe we've met." Jo thrust her hand out. "I'm Joanna Pepperdine, owner of *Divine Bakeshop* and *Second Chance Mercantile*."

The woman stared at her hand for a brief moment and then grudgingly shook it. "Janet Ferris. I'm training Sherry."

Jo attempted to smooth things over. "I'm sorry about Sherry's uniform. It's my fault. I was in a hurry to leave and took off before she had time to make sure she had her things."

"Huh." The woman's frown deepened, and Jo felt sorry for Sherry having to deal with the trainer's attitude. "Is Marlee around?"

"She'll be here shortly."

"I see."

Sherry returned, dressed in her uniform.

"I'll see you after your shift ends," Jo said.

"Thanks."

Jo returned to her vehicle, making a mental note to question Marlee later about Janet. She wasn't sure if the woman was resentful for having to train Sherry or if she was just having a bad day.

Back at the farm, she found Delta in the kitchen.

"...and we all get to try Delta's dessert...yes, we all get to try Delta's Divine dessert..."

Jo tiptoed into the kitchen and peered over her friend's shoulder. "What are you singing?"

"Huh?" Delta tossed a dishtowel over the top of the bowl on the counter. "I didn't hear you come in. You can't be looking at my ingredients...this recipe is top secret."

"Oh, brother." Jo shook her head at her best friend, Delta Childress. "Is it possible you're going a tad overboard with this competition?"

"Joanna Pepperdine, you know that winning the *Divine Fall Festival Baking Contest* could put our bakeshop on the map."

Fall had finally arrived in the small town of Divine, Kansas. It was Jo's first year as a resident of the area, and she was looking forward to the change in the seasons. Having lived in New York City a good deal of her adult life, Jo was no longer accustomed to enjoying nature decked out in its finest.

As of late, the buzz around town revolved around the fall festival and the harvest season. Delta, a former prison cook, and now Jo's cook had decided to enter the competition.

She'd spent the last several days experimenting on an array of recipes...from mile high pies to decadent desserts.

Fortunately, for Jo, she, along with Nash, her handyman, and Gary, the gardener, were her official taste-testers. Although each of them had assured Delta every recipe was contest-worthy, so far none had passed her strict standards.

"They flock to our stores as it is." Jo wagged her finger at her friend. "You're not fooling me. You're determined to beat Marlee."

"Winning is an added bonus. Besides, Marlee has won the last two years. Not that Marlee isn't a good cook, but it's time for a new reigning champion."

"And you aim to be it," Jo said. "I suppose friendly competition is healthy. Will you at least tell me what you're making?"

"Not yet. I'm still perfecting the recipe." Delta returned to her mixing bowl. "How is Sherry's new job at the deli working out?"

"It's too soon to tell, but I think she's having some conflict with the woman who is training her, at least I suspect that's the case."

"You gonna mention it to Marlee?"

"Maybe. On the one hand, I want to help but sometimes butting in only makes matters worse."

"True. Perhaps you should let Sherry bring it up," Delta wisely advised.

Jo offered to help Delta in the kitchen, but she declined, assuring her that her assistant for the day was taking a break and would be returning soon to start working on lunch, so Jo wandered into her office to handle some paperwork.

The morning flew by until Tara, Jo's newest resident, appeared in the doorway, a brown bag in hand. "Delta said you were working and thought you might want to eat your lunch in here."

"Thank you, Tara." Jo motioned her into the office and waited for her to set the bag of food on the desk. "Are you enjoying life on the farm?"

"It's okay. All of the other women are super nice. So far, I've helped Delta in the kitchen and Nash in the workshop. Tomorrow, Kelli will be training me in the mercantile."

"Is there something that would make life better than okay?"

"No." Tara shifted her feet. "It's just…"

"Just what," Jo prompted.

"Well. It's kind of boring, being out here in the middle of nowhere." The young woman hurried on. "I'm more of a city girl."

"I see. The country isn't for everyone."

"It wasn't meant as a complaint." Tara nervously clasped her hands.

"I didn't take it as such." Jo unfolded the top of the bag and reached inside. "You know my door is always open if you need to talk."

"Thank you. I'll keep it in mind." Tara backed out of the office. "I better get back to the kitchen."

Tara left, and Jo ate her food while she continued working, her mind wandering to Sherry and the trainer's unhappy attitude.

After finishing, Jo carried her leftovers into an empty kitchen. She could hear the echo of voices through the back door and found Tara and Delta inspecting one of the raspberry bushes. "I'm on my way to pick up Sherry."

When Jo reached the deli, she headed inside where she spied Sherry filling the salt and pepper shakers. "Hi, Sherry. I'm sorry if I'm late."

"You're right on time." Sherry gave Jo a small smile. "I still have a few more minutes left before clocking out."

"I'll run back and say 'hello' to Marlee." Jo wandered to the kitchen where she found her friend buzzing back and forth.

"Hey, Jo." Marlee stepped over to the pick-up station. "Sherry is somewhere around here."

"She's in the dining room. How did it go today?"

Marlee swiped a strand of hair from her eyes and motioned to Jo. "So-so. Do you have a minute?"

"Sure." Jo cast a quick glance behind her before following Marlee through the kitchen and onto the back patio. "I take it all is not peachy-keen."

"No." Marlee waited for the door to close behind them. "Unfortunately, it's not."

Chapter 2

"Sherry is a dream to work with," Marlee said. "She's a quick learner and very polite. The problem is with the woman training her."

"Janet. She doesn't like Sherry." Jo briefly explained how she'd returned to the deli earlier because Sherry had forgotten her backpack and work uniform. "I wasn't going to say anything but Janet was getting onto her."

"I'm not surprised." Marlee wrinkled her nose. "I caught Janet chewing Sherry out for forgetting to add packets of crackers to the side of a soup bowl, and then another instance where she told Sherry she transposed some numbers on a ticket and rang it up wrong. I finally stepped in and reminded Janet that Sherry was a new employee and that was why she was training her."

"Did you talk to Sherry about it?"

"Yes. She blew it off. My theory is she doesn't want to stir up trouble. I'm going to ask one of the other servers to take over Sherry's training starting tomorrow." Marlee pressed a hand to her forehead. "Janet has always been a difficult employee, but she's good at what she does, which is why I asked her to train Sherry."

"So Janet is a full-time employee?" Jo asked.

"No. She's also a part-timer. She has a second job working part-time at *Four Corners Mini-Mart.*"

"The gas station?"

"Yes." Marlee sighed heavily. "She's been a pain in the butt lately, showing up late for her shifts. I've even gotten a couple of customer complaints about her rudeness."

"Imagine that," Jo murmured.

"I'm going to have a chat with her about her attitude."

"What if Janet thinks Sherry complained about her?" Jo asked. "Maybe you could tell her that I overheard her talking down to her. That way, it's not on Sherry."

"I see your point. Either way, I'm going to put her on notice that her attitude better change, and quick." Marlee clasped her hands. "Are you sure you can't spare a couple more of the women during their off hours?"

Jo chuckled. "Let's see how Sherry does after her training period ends, and then we'll talk about it."

"I figured it couldn't hurt to ask." Marlee changed the subject. "How is Delta doing on her contest dishes?"

"Oh no." Jo shook her head. "You're not dragging me into the middle of your friendly little competition. I'm staying out of it."

"But you are taste-testing for her."

"I am, but I've been sworn to secrecy." Jo made a zipping motion across her lips. "Delta would kill me if she thought I was breathing a hint of what she's been working on."

"Fine. I don't blame Delta. I barely squeaked through with a win last year. I'm keeping my recipes close to the vest, too." Marlee opened the screen door and followed Jo back inside the kitchen. A man wearing a chef's uniform stood near the prep sink. "In fact, I had all of my employees sign an NDA."

"A non-disclosure agreement?" Jo laughed.

"This is serious stuff. There's a trophy, a thousand dollar cash prize award and, of course, all of the prestige."

"I love you both dearly, and I hope the best baker wins." Jo patted her friend's arm.

The man turned the water off. "Marlee made me sign an NDA, too."

"Jo, this is my cook, Carlos."

The man reached for a dishtowel and then shook Jo's hand. "You are the infamous Josephine Pepperdine."

"Joanna...Jo to my friends." Jo smiled. "Hopefully, I'm not too infamous."

"In a good way." The man released his grip.

"It's nice to meet you, Carlos. I'm sure Sherry is out front waiting. I better get going."

Jo waited until they had left the deli to question Sherry. "So how did work go today? Did you do good on your tips?"

"Yes. I made almost fifty bucks. I'm stashing the cash in my medicine cabinet and plan to deposit most of it in my account at *Divine Savings & Loan* during my break tomorrow."

"That's wonderful. How is your training going? Will you be working on your own soon?"

"I hope so." Sherry lowered her gaze and stared at her hands. "I like working with Marlee...of course, not as much as I like working with you."

"It's okay." Jo smiled. "You can like Marlee. She's a nice person. What about the others?" She didn't mention her conversation with Marlee about the other employee, Janet.

"They're...nice. Brenda, one of the other servers, has been helpful and so has Kevin, the busboy."

"What about Janet, the woman who's been training you?"

"I...don't think she likes training me." Sherry hurried on. "I keep forgetting stuff, and I think she's getting irritated. Well, most of the mistakes have been mine. Janet messed up an order and blamed it on me."

"But you're still in training," Jo said gently. "Marlee said you're doing a great job."

"She did?" Sherry's eyes lit.

"Yes. In fact, you're doing such a great job she wondered if any of the other residents might be interested in working at the deli."

"I thought…" Sherry's voice trailed off.

"You thought because Janet didn't like you that Marlee wouldn't."

The woman nodded.

"Well, then you're wrong. You're a model employee, a model resident, Sherry. I've never heard a single complaint from customers at the mercantile or bakeshop. Gary, Delta and Nash all think you do a good job and now Marlee does, too. Promise me you're not going to let one bad apple cause you to doubt yourself."

Sherry shrugged.

"Promise?"

"I promise."

"That's more like it, and remember I'm always here if you need to talk, vent or whatever."

"I don't know what I ever did to deserve finding a home in Divine and at *Second Chance,* but whatever it was, I'm glad."

"I'm glad, too."

When they reached the farm, Sherry headed to her place to drop off her things. She told Jo she grabbed a bite to eat during her break at the deli and planned to track Gary down to see if he needed help in the gardens before dinner.

Jo waited until Sherry rounded the side of the building before climbing the back steps and making her way into the kitchen. The lingering aroma of baked bread filled the kitchen. Delta was nowhere in sight.

"Duke?" Jo called for her hound who was also MIA. She wandered through the dining room and into the living room where she heard the tinkle of Delta's laughter coming from the front porch.

Delta and Gary were on the front porch swing, a snoozing Duke sandwiched between them.

"There you are." Jo pushed the screen door open.

Gary jumped to his feet. "Hello, Jo."

"Hi, Gary. You don't need to get up on my account. Did Delta corner you to try some of the goodies she's been working on for the baking contest?"

"Yes, she did." Gary patted his stomach. "Delta is not only a beautiful woman, but she's a fine cook."

"Oh, Gary." Color flooded Delta's cheeks. "Now don't go trying to butter me up so I'll make more of my chocolate chip banana nut muffins."

"I wouldn't do that." Gary gave Delta a goofy grin before slowly making his way to the steps. "I best run back to the gardens and grab my gardening tools."

"Sherry is on her way there to help you."

"Then I better hurry." He tromped down the steps, across the driveway and out of sight.

Delta stood. "I need to get back in the kitchen. How did Sherry's shift go? Did she have any more trouble with her trainer?"

"As a matter of fact, Marlee brought it up. She said the other employee was giving Sherry a hard time."

"Did she say why?"

"She caught the woman reprimanding her for small mistakes. I asked Sherry about it on the way home. She admitted the woman wasn't happy about having to train her." Jo sighed. "Reading between the lines, I think she has a problem with Sherry, and I'm not sure why. Marlee said she's doing a good job."

"Then that's the woman's problem, not Sherry's."

"I couldn't agree more. Marlee said she's going to have someone else finish training Sherry, so hopefully, this is the end of it." Jo slipped her arm through Delta's and led her to the porch door.

"Marlee tried to get me to spill the beans on what you're working on for the contest."

"That sly fox. You didn't tell her, did you?"

"Not a peep." Jo held the front door and motioned Delta inside. "She also told me she had her employees sign a non-disclosure agreement."

"What?" Delta gasped. "A non-disclosure agreement? Why didn't I think of that?"

"Because Nash, Gary and I would never share your secret recipes," Jo chuckled.

"Well, Marlee just inched this competition up a notch. If she's having them sign NDAs, she must think she has a winning recipe."

"And you have several."

"This will never do." Delta hustled into the kitchen. She threw the kitchen cabinet open and began snatching spices from the rack. "I bet she's making her double chocolate crunch cake. If she is, she's a shoo-in to win."

"No, she's not a shoo-in to win. You are both wonderful bakers, and cooks. You have as much of a chance to win as Marlee does." Jo attempted to reassure Delta that her recipes were just as good, but no matter what she said, it only made her friend work even faster.

She finally gave up and headed to the mercantile to check on the women. By the time she returned, Delta had calmed down.

Dinner consisted of leftovers from the night before. As soon as dinner ended and the table was cleared, Delta was back at it, working on her recipes.

The women, anxious to stay out of Delta's way, headed to their apartments, everyone except for Sherry who lingered behind.

"Is everything all right?" Jo could tell something was troubling the woman.

"Yes. I was thinking about the job at the deli."

"Let's talk in my office." Jo waited until they were inside and then closed the door behind them. "Are you unhappy working there?"

"No." Sherry perched on the edge of the chair looking uncomfortable. "I...it's nothing." She abruptly stood.

"Are you sure?"

"No. I...it's fine." She gave Jo a shy smile. "My shift at the deli is from nine until one-thirty."

"That will give us enough time to eat breakfast before you have to head to work."

"Thanks, Jo."

"You're welcome." Jo's heart sank as she watched Sherry trudge out of her office.

The exchange weighed heavy on Jo's mind for the rest of the evening. Sherry had seemed excited about the job, earning some extra money and most importantly, slowly re-entering the workforce after spending several years locked up in a women's penitentiary. Perhaps it was too much, too fast.

Before drifting off to sleep that night, Jo made a mental note to have Marlee keep an eye on her and to let her know if her new employee was showing signs of stress.

*****

The next morning, Sherry was back to her usual self, cheerful and eager to start her workday. When they reached the deli, she made sure she grabbed her backpack before hopping out of the SUV. She gave Jo a cheery wave and darted inside.

Jo watched her through the windshield, praying God would be with her and give her the self-confidence she so desperately needed, that Marlee would remember her promise to have someone other than Janet train her and she would have a good day.

She pulled out of the parking spot and noticed festive fall banners affixed to each of the downtown lampposts. Smiling jack-o'-lanterns decorated the posts, announcing the upcoming festivities.

The deli and Sherry were forgotten after she returned home and began the tedious task of inventorying the mercantile merchandise.

She devoured a quick lunch while standing at the kitchen counter. Jo rinsed her dirty dishes and started to head back to finish the inventory. She was halfway across the parking lot when her cell phone rang. It was Marlee.

"Hey, Marlee."

"Hey, Jo. I'm sorry to bother you. I need you to come down to the deli right away. I'll explain why when you get here."

Chapter 3

"I'm on my way." Jo grabbed her purse and headed for the door.

She passed Delta, who was on her way back to the house after dropping baked goods off at the bakeshop. "Where are you going? I thought Sherry didn't get out of work until one-thirty."

"I just spoke with Marlee. She asked me to come to the deli right away. I have a feeling it has something to do with Sherry."

"I'll go with you." Delta darted inside to drop off the dishes and ran back to the vehicle. "I hope the woman who was training her..."

"Janet," Jo said.

"Janet?" Delta slammed the door shut. "Oh, I've heard about her. She's trouble. I'm not sure why Marlee has kept that woman on."

"She said pretty much the same thing."

"My niece, Patti, is friends with the owner of the mini-mart. Janet works there part-time, too. She's a troublemaker. In fact, Patti's friend offered her a job just so she could fire Janet."

"You don't say." Jo tightened her grip on the steering wheel, her expression grim. Somehow, she had a sinking feeling Marlee's frantic call had everything to do with Janet.

Her heart plummeted when she turned onto Main Street and discovered several police cars parked in front of the deli. "Uh-oh." Jo circled the block twice before she found an empty spot near the park at the end of the street.

Delta and Jo hustled down the sidewalk and then across the street. A uniformed officer stood blocking the front entrance. "The deli is closed."

"One of my residents, Sherry Marshall, is an employee. The owner, Marlee, called to ask me to come here."

"You are..."

"Joanna Pepperdine."

The man motioned for them to stay put. "I'll be right back." He stepped inside and returned moments later. "I'm sorry. You're going to have to come back later."

"But..."

The officer shook his head.

"Let's go." Delta placed a light hand under Jo's elbow and propelled her down the sidewalk.

"I wonder if I should text Marlee." Jo reached for her cell phone.

"Wait a minute." Delta's arm shot out, almost clotheslining Jo. "I have an idea." She grabbed her friend's hand and dragged her down a small alley, which ran parallel to Main Street. "We're going to sneak around back."

The women hurried to the end of the building. They took a right, zigzagging along a gravel walkway until they were directly behind the building and the employee parking area.

A cluster of police officers was gathered around a small vehicle. Parked next to the vehicle was an ambulance.

Jo's stomach lurched. "Sherry!" She ran toward the officers, her only thought that Sherry was injured. She didn't stop running until she reached the parking area.

Another officer stepped to the side, blocking Jo's path. "This area is off limits."

"My resident, Sherry...the owner called and asked me to come right down here," Jo babbled.

Delta caught up with Jo. "If we can't get any closer, would you please see if Marlee Davison, the owner, or her employee, Sherry, is available?"

"There she is." Delta caught a glimpse of Sherry standing near the deli's back door. Marlee was standing next to her. "I see Marlee and Sherry."

"Where?" Jo craned her neck, eager to catch a glimpse of them. "Yes. I see them now." She pressed a hand to her chest. "Thank you, God."

"Now that we can see they're okay, we'll wait right here," Delta promised.

The officer gave them a curt nod before joining the others.

Delta waited until the officer's back was turned before waving her arms in an attempt to catch Marlee or Sherry's eye. Finally, Sherry glanced in their direction. She hurried over, her expression pinched.

"What's going on?" Jo asked. "Marlee called. She sounded frantic and asked me to come down here. I thought something happened to you."

"Not me. Janet."

"Janet, as in the employee who was training you, Janet?" Jo asked.

"Yes. We got into an argument. She said something about quitting and then stormed out. I told Marlee what happened and she told me not to worry about it."

Sherry shot a quick glance behind her. "When she didn't come back, Marlee and I figured she made good on her threat. Kevin, the busboy, came out back to empty the trash. He spotted Janet's car and ran inside to tell Marlee she was still here. That's when Marlee found her."

"Found Janet," Delta prompted.

"She's dead."

Jo made a gurgling noise. "Dead?"

"I don't know what happened. The cops got here fast. When they found out Janet and I argued earlier, they started asking me a bunch of questions. They talked to Brenda, the other server, along with the cook, Carlos and Marlee."

"Surely, they can't believe you were responsible for the woman's death," Jo said. "You were working."

"Not the entire time." Sherry clasped her hands, twining her fingers tightly together. "I ran down to the bank on my break, to deposit my tip money."

"I'm sure the bank gave you a time-stamped receipt."

"They did. I kept a little spending money out, so after I made my deposit, I stopped by the Twistee Treat for a smoothie. I spent the rest of my morning break in the park."

"Because you wanted to avoid another run-in with Janet if she came back," Jo guessed.

"Yep." Sherry sucked in a breath and nodded.

"I can't believe this." Jo began pacing.

"You believe me? I didn't take her out."

Jo abruptly stopped. "Of course I believe you, Sherry."

"We don't know how she died," Delta pointed out. "It could be she died of natural causes."

"Right," Jo agreed. "Perhaps she was emotionally unstable and committed suicide."

"Here comes Marlee."

Marlee made her way over, her face bore the same expression as Sherry's. "The investigators won't let you get any closer?"

"No. Sherry told us what happened, how she argued with Janet and the woman threatened to quit before storming out." Jo motioned to the vehicle. "Is Janet still inside the car?"

"Yes. I think they're going to take her away...soon," Marlee said. "I better get back there. I want to hear what they're saying."

"I'll go with you." Sherry turned to Jo. "I'll call you when the authorities are done questioning me."

"Hang in there." Jo squeezed Sherry's arm. "It's going to be all right. You know you had nothing to

33

do with Janet's death. We know you had nothing to do with her death."

Sherry nodded, but Jo could tell by the look on her face she wasn't convinced. Even without having done anything wrong, being a convicted felon was a major strike against her.

If the investigators suspected foul play, Sherry would have to work hard to prove her innocence. The fact she had taken a break after the woman stormed out was concerning.

Delta and Jo slowly made their way back to the SUV. "I hate to say it, but if the woman's death is suspicious, Sherry will be the investigator's number one suspect."

"Motive and opportunity," Jo grimaced. "If what you said was true, she wasn't well-liked by her co-workers, both here and at the mini-mart."

"Speaking of mini-mart, with all of these extra trips to town, the SUV is getting low on gas. We'll stop by there on our way home."

When they reached the mini-mart, Jo pumped the gas while Delta ran inside to grab a couple of sodas. She was replacing the gas nozzle when her friend returned. "Whew! What a mess."

"Mess?" Jo reached for her receipt.

"Janet went on a rampage before she died."

"Inside the gas station?"

"Yeah. From what I heard, it looks like Janet worked at the deli first thing this morning, training Sherry. After she and Sherry argued, Janet stormed out of the deli and drove here. She got into it with a co-worker and went berserk."

"What set her off?"

"I don't know. The worker inside didn't know, either. After she freaked out, Janet tore out of there."

"She must've gone back to the deli," Jo theorized.

"Right. Maybe to confront Sherry or Marlee, but she never made it that far."

"Could be she got herself so worked up, she had a heart attack." Jo started the SUV and waited for Delta to buckle up. During the trip home, Delta and Jo discussed the disturbing events.

"This is all speculation," Delta said. "We'll have to wait for more information."

"Hopefully, we'll hear from Marlee or Sherry soon." Back home, Jo made sure she had her cell phone with her before returning to the mercantile to finish her final inventory.

The store was busy for a Wednesday afternoon. She gave Kelli, who was working the cash register, a quick wave and made her way to the back.

Kelli followed her to the storage area. "Hey, Jo. I was looking for you earlier."

"I had to make a quick trip into town." Jo almost mentioned the crisis at the deli but decided to hold off until they knew more. "Did you need me?"

"There was a man in here earlier looking for you."

Jo dropped the shirt she was holding. "Was there an issue with one of our customers?"

"No. I don't think he was a customer. I watched him walk in. He came right to the counter and asked if Joanna Pepperdine was the owner. I told him 'yes,' and then he asked if he could have a word with you. I sent Leah to the house to track you down, and that's when we realized you had left."

"What did he say when you told him I wasn't here?"

"He said he would stop back later. Maybe it was someone from the county finally coming to investigate the claim that you're running an unlicensed bed and breakfast," Kelli said.

"No, that case was closed, and no one else is after us." Jo attempted to lighten the mood. "At least not that I'm aware of."

"Right," Kelli nodded. "Well, I better get back to work."

Jo thanked her for the heads up and began working through the last of the clothing inventory, her thoughts on Sherry. She checked her cell phone several times, waiting for the call.

Jo finished her task and headed to the bakeshop to check on Michelle, another resident who was working.

"We already ran out of our peanut butter delight cookies."

"How are our produce sales?"

Ever since Nash had come up with the brilliant idea to add wheelbarrow produce displays to the shop, sales had tripled, and Jo was thrilled.

With harvest season in full swing, they had a bountiful supply of garden goodies and the extra income was helping build a comfortable nest egg for the coming winter months when business slowed.

"We're selling almost as much produce as we are baked goods."

"Awesome," Jo beamed. "That's great news." She turned to go and nearly collided with a man standing directly behind her.

"Joanna Pepperdine?"

"Yes. I'm Joanna Pepperdine."

"Finally, we meet." A slow smile spread across the man's face. "You're a hard woman to track down."

"I didn't know anyone was looking for me," Jo quipped.

"If you have a moment...could we step outside?"

"Of course." There was something about the man's demeanor and the tone of his voice that sent up red flags. Jo forced a smile and led him out of the bakeshop. They stopped when they reached the end of the walkway.

"I can see I caught you off guard." The man reached into his jacket pocket. He pulled out a business card and handed it to Jo:

Neil Garland, Detective
All Points Investigative Services
Serving the Greater Wichita Area.

Jo studied the card. "You're a private investigator. What do you want with me?"

Instead of answering Jo's question, the detective asked one of his own. "You are Joanna *Carlton* Pepperdine?"

Jo's blood ran cold...her past, the past she'd fought so hard to put behind her, was staring her directly in the face.

Chapter 4

"I'm Joanna Carlton Pepperdine. Who's asking?"

"Miles Parker. Does the name ring a bell?"

"No. I've never met anyone by the name of Miles Parker unless he shops here at the bakeshop or mercantile and I never knew his name."

The detective slipped his hands in his front pockets. "Miles lives in California. His mother's name was Irene Parker. She was originally from the Wichita area."

The man looked at her expectantly, as if waiting for a flicker of recognition to register.

Frustrated, Jo shook her head. "You're talking in circles. I have no idea who Miles or Irene Parker might be. So you know my full name...Joanna

Carlton Pepperdine. My parents are deceased. I have no siblings or close relatives."

"Now that is where I come in and where you are wrong. Mr. Parker hired me to find you. He claims to be a relative..." Garland rocked back on his heels. "That is all I'm authorized to say, and now that I've found you, my job here is done."

The man turned to go, and Jo's hand shot out to stop him. "That's it? You show up on my doorstep, claiming you were hired by this mysterious Parker person and I have family I know nothing about."

"As I said, I was hired to find you, and that is what I've done." The detective's eyes slowly scanned the surroundings. "You have quite a set up here. I did a little background research. You run a halfway house for former convicts from the *Central State Women's Penitentiary*, a place you're familiar with."

He took a slow step back, and Jo let her hand fall to her side. "I have to say I'm surprised a woman of your wealth would use her massive resources to house a bunch of criminals."

"They are not criminals. These women are former convicts who have done their time and deserve a second chance."

"How noble of you," the man mocked. "I'm sure it helps to assuage some of the guilt associated with your wealth. Although I think I would rather deal with my guilt by purchasing a private island somewhere in the Caribbean, where I could sip fruity drinks all day and count my millions."

"Thank you for your unsolicited opinion." Despite her aggravation, Jo was growing more concerned by the minute. Someone was looking for her...someone who knew her secret and her past. "If you're through, I have a business to run."

"Oh, I am. Like I said, my job here is done. As for Mr. Parker? Well, I'm sure he'll be in touch." The man left the threat hanging in the air. He turned on his heel and made his way to an expensive sports car parked out front.

Jo watched him pull out of the drive and disappear from sight. She stood there for a long time, staring blankly at the road.

Miles Parker had taken the time to hire a private investigator to track Jo down. Who was Parker and why would the investigator think she might have a clue to who he was?

A relative? Jo quickly dismissed the thought. She was an only child. She had an uncle, Maurice Carlton, on her father's side. He lived in Texas and had a daughter, Eadie, who was Jo's cousin.

As far as her mother's side, like Jo, she was an only child and her maiden name was Holden. Perhaps this man was lying. Someone somewhere had found out about Jo's past and planned to lay claim to her fortune.

They would have a hard time. Jo had plenty of resources to hire the best attorneys money could buy. She forced the man's disturbing visit from her mind and returned to the house.

In no mood to talk, she crept into her office and quietly closed the door behind her. Jo eased in behind the desk and turned her computer on but had trouble focusing.

She was troubled not only by the investigator's arrival; she was concerned about the death at the deli. She glanced at the clock. It was after three now, and there was still no word from Sherry or Marlee.

Restless, Jo turned her computer off and wandered into the kitchen. She found Delta standing in front of the kitchen counter staring at an array of clear plastic storage containers.

"What are you doing?"

"The most frustrating chore I can think of...tracking down missing lids." Delta waved a plastic cover in the air. "Every time I turn around, another one comes up missing. I swear these lids have legs and run off in the middle of the night."

"Almost like socks in the laundry." Jo grabbed a pitcher of tea from the fridge and poured a glass.

Delta turned her attention back to the storage containers while Jo began tapping her foot on the linoleum.

"Joanna Pepperdine."

"What?"

Delta turned, giving Jo her full attention. "What is wrong? You're a million miles away not to mention you're wearing a hole in my floor."

"Sorry." Jo slid into an empty chair. "I have a lot on my mind."

"So do I. I'm thinking about setting up a surveillance camera in the kitchen to find out what keeps happening to my lids," Delta joked.

Jo didn't answer.

"Jo." Delta crossed the room and waved a hand in front of Jo's face. "Earth to Jo."

"I'm sorry, did you say something?"

"I said I've decided to enter baked roadkill skunk in the contest. I'm sure no one else is gonna serve skunk."

"That's a great idea."

"That's what I thought. You haven't listened to a single word I said."

"I'm sorry." Jo mentally shook her head and turned to Delta. "You're right."

"Don't worry about Sherry."

"I'm not worried about Sherry. I take that back. I'm also worried about Sherry."

"I missed something," Delta said. "Are you gonna tell me what's got you so discombobulated?"

"The thought of eating skunk stew," Jo teased.

"Very funny. So what's up?"

"A private investigator from Wichita showed up at the bakeshop. He knows."

"Knows what?"

"He knows my name...Joanna Carlton Pepperdine. He knows about the women's penitentiary. He knows about my money."

"So what? You haven't done anything wrong."

"He claims he was hired by a relative, Miles Parker," Jo said.

"Who is Miles Parker?"

"I have no idea. I've never heard the name before in my life."

"People find out you have money." Delta snapped her fingers. "They come out of the woodwork. I'm surprised it has taken this long for a long-lost relative to track you down."

"True. I'm sure it's someone my parents knew, someone who decided they needed money and is now claiming we're related."

"You have nothing to worry about. We have enough on our plates. Besides, you have plenty of money to fight off any claims someone might bring about."

"But they went to all of the trouble to hire a detective to track me down...after all of this time. Why now?"

"Who knows," Delta shrugged. "We'll have to wait to see if...or when this mysterious Miles Parker shows up. For now, I give up on the lid project. It's time to start working on a sample baked bacon cheese dip."

"I thought this was a baking contest."

"It is," Delta said. "I got my hands on a copy of the contest rules. Nowhere does it say it has to be a pastry, pie, cake or bread. In fact, the only requirements are that it's made from scratch and baked in the oven, so I can make whatever I want."

The women assembled the ingredients and began working on the dip when Jo's cell phone beeped. It was a message from Marlee telling Jo the investigators had finished questioning Sherry, and she was ready to go.

"I better pick her up before they change their mind." Jo untied her apron and hung it on the hook.

"Do you want me to go with you?" Delta asked.

"No. I'll give you a call if I run into a problem."

Jo returned to town and the deli. The police cars were gone. The sign on the door said closed, but when Jo tried the door, it was unlocked. She crossed through the dining room and made her way to the kitchen.

Marlee, along with Sherry and two other people Jo recognized as employees, had gathered in the back. The expressions on their faces were somber.

"The investigators are gone. I take it they were able to give you some idea about what happened to Janet."

"Yes," Marlee nodded. "You're not going to believe this."

Chapter 5

"Janet told several people that she and Sherry weren't getting along. She told them Sherry threatened her and she feared for her life because Sherry was a former convict."

"Th-that's absurd," Jo turned to her resident. "Did you threaten Janet?"

"I told her I was going to report her for using her cell phone during working hours," Sherry said. "If you call that a threat."

"Was she using her cell phone?" Jo asked.

"Yes. She was sneaking into the employee breakroom with her phone, which is why she became aggravated with me. Janet wanted me to handle all of her work while she kept all of the tips and texted. She also blamed me for mixing up an order when she was the one who wrote it."

"They finally took Janet away and towed her car." Marlee went on to explain the investigators questioned her, along with all of the other deli employees extensively, as well as the customers in the restaurant. "They took Janet's purse and her personal belongings."

"And I'm sure they searched all of the other employees' belongings, too," Jo said.

"They did. At least they're gone now and Sherry is free to leave."

"I'm ready to go," Sherry said.

"I don't blame you. I must admit, it has been a long day and it's not even over yet." Jo thought about the private investigator who showed up on her doorstep earlier.

"I'll go grab my things."

Marlee waited for Sherry to step out of the kitchen before motioning Jo to the server station, away from the other employees. "I don't want to scare Sherry, but I have a bad feeling about this. The investigators were downright badgering her, almost like an interrogation."

"They think Sherry is somehow involved in Janet's death."

"That's the impression I got." Marlee pressed a hand to her chest. "I'm so sorry, Jo. I knew Janet was giving Sherry a hard time. I planned to ask one of the other servers to finish training her this morning but it's been so crazy busy, I never got around to it."

"You can't blame yourself. I know Sherry didn't harm Janet. It's only a matter of time before the authorities reach the same conclusion."

"I hope so. Do you think Sherry will still want to work here?"

"Do you still want her?" Jo pointed out the townsfolks might not be keen on eating at the deli if one of Marlee's employees was a suspect in a murder investigation.

"Of course. Besides, we still don't know the cause of Janet's death. It could be suicide or natural causes. There's no sense in panicking until we have more information."

Sherry joined them, carrying her backpack.

"Could you come in tomorrow morning?" Marlee asked. "I'm going to be a little short-staffed."

"Do you still want me?" Sherry looked surprised. "I figured you wouldn't want me back here."

"Absolutely." Marlee nodded firmly. "You're a great employee, Sherry. In fact, you're darn near perfect. So can you come in to cover a breakfast shift?"

"Yes." Sherry's head bobbed up and down. "I...thank you, Marlee. Thank you for believing me."

"Thank *you* for not quitting." Marlee walked Jo and Sherry to the front door and then turned the sign to *Open*.

Several diners, who were waiting on the sidewalk, headed in while Sherry and Jo headed out.

"It doesn't look like the employee's death is going to hurt Marlee's business."

"I'm glad." Sherry tossed her backpack on the floor and climbed in the passenger seat. "I should've kept my mouth shut when Janet got in my face."

"You had a natural reaction," Jo said. "Besides, it sounds like Janet overreacted and Marlee needed to know she wasn't doing her job."

"Right." Sherry silently stared out the window on the way home.

Jo could see the woman was worried about the death, not that she could blame her. The fact that Janet had told people Sherry threatened her and she was frightened of her only hours before her death was concerning.

Sherry waited until they were home to speak. "I'm going to drop my things off and then start my short shift in the bakeshop."

"I'll see you at dinner."

Sherry turned to go.

"Hey." Jo stopped her. "Hold your head up. We're going to pray about it at dinner. God has this under control."

"Thanks, Jo. I hope so." Sherry attempted a smile that didn't quite make it. With shoulders slumped, she trudged across the drive and disappeared behind the back of the building.

Jo's first stop was the kitchen. It was empty, but the door leading to the cellar was wide open. "Delta?"

Delta appeared at the bottom of the stairs.

"What're you doing?"

"Gary helped me sort through the canning jars. I'm gonna clean them so we can start canning." Delta, her arms laden with glass jars, climbed the stairs.

"I'll help." Jo darted down the stairs. She gathered an armful of jars and carried them up the steps. "What do you plan to can?"

Delta rattled off her list. "I'm starting with tomatoes, sweet pickles, dill pickles and corn. I'll fill these jars before you know it. How's Sherry?"

"Not good." Jo briefly explained what had transpired at the deli, how Janet and Sherry had argued. Janet had also told several others Sherry had threatened her and she was afraid of her.

"Threatened her?" Delta interrupted.

"According to Sherry, she threatened to report Janet to Marlee for using her cell phone during working hours. The investigators searched the deli, questioned the employees and then left with Janet, her belongings and her car. We still don't know the cause of death."

"So it could be accidental or due to natural causes."

"I hope so. I told Sherry we would pray about it at dinner."

"What does Marlee think?" Delta set the jars in the kitchen sink and began filling them with water.

"That Sherry is innocent, and the authorities will figure out what happened to Janet. In fact, she's asked Sherry to come in a little early tomorrow. She said she's a model employee."

"Then we have nothing to worry about."

The rest of the afternoon passed quickly with Jo half-expecting Miles Parker to show up at any moment. When he didn't show, she began to relax.

The evening dinner was a somber event after Jo explained to the other women about Sherry's run-in with a co-worker and the woman's sudden death. "We need to pray for Sherry tonight."

Jo made a point of saying a special prayer each evening for one member of the household, whether it was one of the female residents, Nash, Delta, Gary or even herself.

Tonight was Sherry's night. The women and Nash grew quiet and bowed their heads.

Jo clasped her hands in her lap. "Dear Lord. We thank you for this wonderful food, for giving us one more day on earth and blessing our home and the businesses. Thank you for bringing each of these special women here. Please fill them with your ever-present peace, joyful hearts, stay close to them and draw them near."

She continued. "Lord, we pray for Janet Ferris, for her family and for your presence in this time of sorrow. We also bring Sherry to you tonight. You know her situation and the uncertainty of the hours or even days ahead as the authorities determine what happened to Janet, Sherry's co-worker. Lord, we pray you uncover the truth, and your will be done."

"Amen." A chorus of voices ended the prayer.

Raylene turned to Sherry, who was seated next to her. "You have an airtight alibi. I don't see how the authorities could suspect you of being responsible for Janet's death."

"Not necessarily. Janet took her break first when she stormed out. When she didn't return, Marlee told me to go ahead and take mine before the lunch crowd arrived. I have a partial alibi. I stopped by the bank to deposit my tip money and then spent the rest of my break in the park."

"We still don't know the cause of death," Jo pointed out. "Marlee thought she might have more information this evening. In fact, I'm going to give her a call after dinner, to see if she's heard anything."

The conversation drifted to their upcoming fall decorating party. Delta and Jo had spent the previous Saturday shopping for fall decorations in the nearby town of Centerpoint Junction.

Jo had splurged, buying stuffed scarecrows, lighted pumpkins, festive balloons and creepy candles decorated with crawly spiders.

The women pored over the goodies they had purchased and were excited about the upcoming *Fall Harvest Festival*. Jo decided to kick it off with their own fall decorating party.

Even Nash had gotten in on the decorating plans, claiming he was working on a special surprise for the fall season, something he would unveil at the party.

If the fall decorating party went smoothly, Jo decided to host another one for the residents for the Christmas season, her favorite holiday, where they would all take part in a gift exchange.

"I have something else I've been working on," Jo announced. "I found a self-defense instructor. Nash has graciously agreed to cover the store and Claire the owner of *Claire's Collectibles*, offered to work at the bakeshop. Her nephew, a former police officer, teaches classes part-time. She pulled some strings, and he's agreed to come here."

"Self-defense?" Delta reached for a roll.

"After our most recent incidents, I decided it wouldn't hurt to have a self-defense course."

"And I agreed," Nash chimed in.

"Then we got ourselves a busy day tomorrow," Delta said.

"The self-defense class starts at five o'clock in the barn. Nash already cleared a spot for us. Dinner will be at six, and then we all get to collapse for the night," Jo joked.

The women helped clear the table while Jo headed to her office to place a call to Marlee.

"Hey, Jo."

"Hello, Marlee. I'm sorry to bother you. I thought I would give you a quick call to see if you've heard anything else about Janet Ferris' death."

"I have. In fact, I was just going to give you a call. The police investigation is heating up."

Chapter 6

Jo's heart sank. "Then Janet's death is suspicious."

"Not only suspicious but it's being investigated as a homicide. She was strangled."

"Strangled?" Jo slumped down into her chair.

"Reading between the lines, the investigators believe someone was hiding in the backseat of Janet's car. When they were alone, the killer attacked and strangled her."

"Right there in the driver's seat?"

"My guess is it happened so fast, Janet didn't have time to lay on the horn or try to escape."

"What a terrible way to go." A horrifying thought filled Jo's mind. "This means the investigators will focus their attention on the *Divine Delicatessen* employees or even the customers."

"Yes. Since it happened on my property, right behind my business. This is awful."

"Let's try to remain calm." Jo said the words but even as she said them, a feeling of dread settled in the pit of her stomach. "It could have been anyone. Earlier, Delta and I stopped by the mini-mart for gas. Delta talked to one of the employees who told her Janet was inside the gas station during her break today, freaking out."

"I heard. The rumors are flying that Janet had some sort of mental breakdown. She stormed into the gas station, threatening the employees before jumping into her car and taking off."

"Where the killer took her out," Jo said.

"In a nutshell." Marlee's voice grew muffled. "Listen, I've got to go. I'll see you in the morning."

"When I drop Sherry off." Jo thanked Marlee for the update and headed back to the kitchen where she found Delta and Raylene, who had a troubled expression on her face. "You have that look, Raylene."

"I didn't want to scare Sherry, but if this woman died a suspicious death, she'll be the number one suspect."

"I'm afraid you're right." Jo almost slipped, revealing Janet's cause of death but kept quiet. The last thing she needed was for word to get back to Sherry. She wanted to break the news to the woman in the morning when they were alone.

Instead, she simply said, "We'll find out soon enough."

"I'm here to help if you need me."

Jo tilted her head, touched by her resident's concern. "I appreciate the offer, Raylene. You're a good friend."

"Would you like to sample one of my loaded cheesecake blondies before you go?" Delta asked. "I was gonna put them out for dessert tonight but forgot."

"Sure," Raylene grinned. "I'll be your guinea pig any day...or night."

Delta grabbed the spatula, eased a piece from the pan and held it out.

Raylene carefully broke off a big chunk before popping it into her mouth. "Oh man...what's in this?"

"Everything but the kitchen sink." Delta rattled off a list of ingredients. "The number one ingredient is cream cheese, plus chocolate chips, along with macadamia nuts." She pinched her thumb and index finger together. "And a pinch of vanilla."

"Delicious." Raylene shoved the rest of the treat in her mouth. "I could eat the whole pan. Thanks, Delta."

"You're welcome. So you think this recipe should be in the running for the contest?"

"Without a doubt. I had better get out of here before I'm tempted to eat more. I can feel the pounds already packing on." Raylene breezed out of the house, whistling a catchy tune.

Delta smiled widely as she watched her leave. "That woman has got a weight lifted off her shoulders. Ever since the vote and she found out she was staying, she's like a new person."

"Isn't it wonderful? Things are looking up for Raylene." Jo sobered. "I spoke to Marlee a few minutes ago. Janet Ferris was strangled inside her vehicle while it was parked behind the deli."

"Oh, dear," Delta gasped. "How awful."

"It is. Do you remember when we stopped at the gas station and the employee told you Janet went on a rampage right before her death?"

"Yes."

"Do you remember who it was that you spoke to?"

"It was a woman. She wasn't the one Janet got into it with. It was someone else. I was just so surprised, I wasn't paying close attention."

"But you would remember what the person looked like...the employee."

"I do. I never forget a face."

"Good. Because I think I'm going to stop by there tomorrow after I drop Sherry off at work."

*****

As soon as Jo finished her breakfast early the next morning, she made a quick trip to the gardens where she found Gary wandering up and down the rows.

"The garden looks wonderful. I don't know how we would survive without your green thumb." Jo pointed to the wire mesh guarding the perimeter. "How is the wire mesh working?"

"Better than I thought it would." Gary stepped over the rows and joined Jo off to the side.

"Michelle told me the produce sales are doing real good these days."

"Yes, thanks to you and Nash." Jo started to say something else when the sound of a combine in the field next door interrupted her. Instead of turning around, the contraption abruptly stopped. A man jumped out of the cab and made his way to the fence line.

"Hello, neighbors." The man gave a friendly wave. "Hello, Gary. You got a nice garden going there."

"Thanks, Dave. Have you met the boss lady?" Gary motioned to Jo.

"Not yet." The tall, thin man smiled as he extended a hand over the top of the fence. "David Kilwin."

Jo returned the smile. "Joanna Pepperdine. Jo to my friends."

"Jo." He took her hand in a warm grip and gave it a firm shake.

Jo studied his face, realizing he looked vaguely familiar. "Are you sure we haven't met before? You look familiar."

Kilwin chuckled. "I'm sure I do. I'm a regular in the bakeshop, scooping up some of Delta's divine baked goods."

"Ah. Now I know where I've seen you." Jo lifted a brow. "You're the coconut cream pie customer."

"Guilty as charged," Kilwin joked. "It's sad to think people remember you by your eating habits."

"Oh...but Delta's pies." Jo patted her stomach.

"Welcome to Divine. I hoped to introduce myself a few weeks ago, but you were gone. One of the bakeshop employees, Kelli, I think, said you were in town running errands."

"The businesses keep me busy."

"I bet they do. Well, I better get back to work." Kilwin motioned to his combine. "The fields are calling."

Gary tugged on his suspenders. "That's a fine piece of machinery."

"Thanks. I snatched this baby up at auction. It's a John Deere S690. I bought it just in time for the fall harvest."

"You gonna take part in the *Divine Harvest Moon Competition?*"

"I'm thinking about it. Couldn't last year because my tractor was on its last leg. I finally had to put the old International out to pasture."

"Well, good luck if you do," Gary said.

"Thanks. I had better get back to it. It was nice to finally officially meet you, neighbor."

"Same here," Jo replied.

Gary waited until Kilwin climbed into his tractor and fired it up. The massive metal machinery shook the ground as it rumbled off. "Speaking of competition, how is Delta doing on narrowing down her entry for the baking contest?"

"Last I heard she was getting close."

"I don't care how long she works on it. I'll taste test until the cows come home," Gary joked. "That woman can surely cook." He changed the subject. "I brought you a few bales of hay for your fall decorating party. I left them in front of Nash's workshop."

"Thanks, Gary. The women are excited about decorating. You're more than welcome to join us. Delta promised to whip up some special treats for the occasion."

"Sure. I would love to join you," Gary beamed. "It sounds like fun."

"I better get going." Jo left Gary to finish tending the gardens and wandered back to the front. The bakeshop and mercantile, both of which had just opened, were already bustling with customers.

Kelli and Leah, along with Tara, the newest resident, assured Jo they had everything under control, so she returned to the house to finish getting ready. Sherry was already dressed and waiting for Jo when she returned downstairs.

"Let's hit the road." Jo waited until they left the farm to mention Janet's death. "I spoke to Marlee last night. The authorities believe Janet was murdered."

"Murdered?"

"She was strangled."

Sherry made a choking sound. "You're kidding."

"Reading between the lines, Marlee thinks someone sneaked into Janet's car and was hiding in the backseat while it was parked behind the deli."

"I...the authorities are going to think I killed her. They're going to arrest me."

Jo forced her voice to remain calm. "No, they're not. You did not kill Janet. The authorities have no proof. They can't arrest you without some sort of proof."

What Jo didn't say was they could still question Sherry, or more like interrogate, in an attempt to coerce a confession.

"They're going to pin it on me." Sherry began shaking her head. "I know how this is going to go down. The investigators are going to pick me up under the guise of asking a few questions, and then they'll drive me to the station and lead me into an interrogation room where they'll come at me nonstop until I confess. I'm going back to prison." She began to cry.

Jo pulled off the road and shifted into park. "You are not going to prison. The authorities are not going to arrest you. Listen..." Jo paused, her mind racing.

Unfortunately, Sherry was right. She knew the drill...all too well. "Listen to me." Jo grasped Sherry's hand. "Look at me."

Sherry lifted her gaze, her eyes meeting Jo's eyes. "Listen to me very carefully. If the authorities show up at the deli to question you, excuse yourself and call me immediately. Hide out in the women's restroom if you have to. Wait there until I can get to you. I don't want you talking to them again unless I'm present."

"But what can you do?"

"I can hire the best lawyer money can buy," Jo said grimly.

"I can't afford an attorney," Sherry whispered.

"You can't, but I can." Jo shifted into drive and glanced in her side mirror before pulling back onto the road. "You must promise me. What are you going to do if the authorities show up and want to talk to you?"

"I'm going to excuse myself, sneak into the back, call you and then hide out in the bathroom until you get there."

"Yes." Jo parked the SUV and followed Sherry inside. They found Marlee in the back, her face a splotchy red and her expression pinched.

"You look like we feel," Jo said.

"It's gonna be a rough one." Marlee strode across the room. "I'm glad you're here, Sherry. I gave this a lot of thought last night. If the authorities show up and want to question you again, we're going to tell them you want an attorney present during questioning."

Despite the seriousness of the situation, Jo smiled. "You must have read my mind. I told Sherry the exact same thing." She told Marlee to call her - that she would drop everything and return to the deli.

"Perfect." Marlee's expression relaxed. "Hopefully, we're way off, and the investigators are working on other leads."

"I hope so, too." Jo gave Sherry a quick hug. "Hang in there. We're going to get through this."

Jo's next stop was *Four Corners Mini-Mart*. Before leaving, Delta had given Jo a detailed description of the employee she'd spoken with the previous day. She started to pull into the gas station, when she spied what she believed was an unmarked police car, along with a Smith County Sheriff's patrol car.

Instead of pulling in, she headed home, making a mental note to stop by later on her way back to town.

When she arrived, she found Delta inside the house, a concerned expression on her face. "Did you stop by the mercantile?"

"No. Why?"

"There's a man over there, waiting to talk to you. He said his name was Miles Parker. Leah told him you weren't here. He told her he had something important to discuss and would wait."

Chapter 7

Jo began to feel lightheaded. She reached out to steady herself. "I had hoped the detective was wrong."

"Maybe you should sit down for a sec."

"I feel like passing out." Jo let Delta lead her to a kitchen chair. "Why after all of these years?"

"Who knows? You also don't know how he claims to be related. Perhaps he's a second cousin or some such nonsense. If that's the case, you'll be polite, offer him a batch of complimentary brownies and send him on his way."

"No." Jo shook her head. "There's no way a distant relative would go to the trouble, not to mention the expense, of hiring a private investigator to find me."

"There's only one way to find out," Delta reached inside the cupboard and grabbed an empty glass. She filled it with water and handed it to Jo. "Would you like me to run next door and bring him here? You'll have more privacy."

"Yes. Yes. I like that idea." Jo's hand trembled as she lifted the glass. "Give me another minute to pull myself together."

"Take all the time you need," Delta said. "He's waited this long to blindside you. A few more minutes ain't gonna kill him."

"Right." Jo slowly sipped the water, her mind whirling. Surely, the man was mistaken. She had no family other than an uncle and a cousin. "I think I'm ready."

"I'll be right back." Delta dashed out the door and Jo watched her go, a sudden pain piercing her chest. She sucked in a breath and began to pray God would help her remain calm.

Creak. The back door creaked open. Jo dropped her hand, willing the chest pains to stop.

Delta appeared first, followed by a man who looked to be in his early forties, his light brown hair short and spiked in the front, giving him a clean-cut look.

He wasn't tall, but then he wasn't short. He was medium build with a slight tan to his complexion. His eyes, a shade of gray-green met Jo's eyes.

Jo pushed the chair back and slowly stood. "Mr. Parker. I heard you wanted to speak with me." She forced her voice to remain cool, her face expressionless.

"Yes, Ms. Pepperdine. You spoke with Neil Garland, my private investigator, yesterday. He briefly explained my reason for tracking you down."

"Not entirely. He said something about a relative." Jo didn't offer her hand, nor did Mr. Parker. "My parents are dead; I have an uncle who lives in Texas and a cousin, Eadie. I have no other relatives."

"That you were aware of." Parker smiled, but the smile never reached his eyes. They were cold and dark, and Jo believed whatever the man was about to tell her would change her life. "You see…you and I have the same father. Andrew Michael Carlton is my father."

Jo started to sway. She grabbed the back of the chair and locked her knees so they wouldn't buckle. She said the first thing that popped into her head. "I think you're mistaken. I have no siblings."

"And that's where *you're* mistaken. Our illustrious father was having an affair with my mother, Irene Parker. She was Andrew's assistant. The affair went on for years, until Mother became pregnant with me. Father paid her off and sent us away to California."

"I don't believe you," Jo whispered. "You're lying."

"Am I?" The man gave Jo a mocking smile. "Because Andrew Carlton was a faithful husband as well as a loving and devoted father?"

"You know nothing about my family or my father."

"Now that is the truth." Parker rocked back on his heels. "I never met dear old Dad, but he was timely in mailing a check to my mother, every month like clockwork until I turned eighteen. She never uttered his name, not once. I guess pops paid her enough to keep quiet."

"How do you know all of this?"

"Because my mother saved every check receipt, every note he ever wrote her while they were together. It wasn't until about a month ago, after she died and I was sorting through her things, that I discovered the truth," Parker said. "Shocking isn't it? You have the same look on your face, the one I had when I found out how truly wealthy Andrew Carlton was...filthy rich. A pillar of Wichita society, a philanthropist."

He paused and Jo could see he was thoroughly enjoying every jab, every stab that pierced her heart. "Imagine my shock when I discovered the founder of *Carlton Oil & Gas Company* was my long-lost parent. And even more surprised when I discovered he was also dead...at the hands of his wife, Jessica Holden Carlton, your mother."

"I don't know who you are...or why you waited until now to show up on my doorstep, other than you are someone looking for some quick cash, but until you can prove otherwise, you need to leave and never step foot on my property again." Jo marched to the back door. She flung it open and motioned the man out. "Get out before I call the police."

Delta, who so far had remained silent, spoke. "Or I go grab one of my guns and shoot you for trespassing."

A flicker of fear crossed the man's face. "You wouldn't dare."

"Don't try me." Delta glared at the man.

"This isn't the last you've heard of me." Parker hurried down the breezeway steps to the backyard. He took several steps back until he was a safe distance from Delta's deadly glare.

"I had a chance to look around before you got here," Parker said. "You have a slick business set up. I took the opportunity to drive around the area, too. I believe I'm going to enjoy living in Divine and running this fine establishment."

"Over my dead body," Jo roared.

"I'm gettin' my gun." Delta ran back inside, and Parker started jogging across the parking lot.

She returned in time to see Parker peel out of the driveway, throwing a spray of gravel as he sped off in his car.

Delta waved her pistol in the air. "Don't ever come back!"

As soon as Miles Parker was out of sight, Jo's knees gave way, and she hit the ground, wrapping her arms around her waist, her forehead pressed against the soft grass.

Miles Parker's taunts brought Jo's past flooding back. She was an adult before she fully grasped the tumultuous and abusive relationship between her parents, although there had always been small signs.

Growing up, Jo's mother, Jessica, dubbed the darling of high society by the local news, hosted the talk of the town gala events at their stately mansion in one of Wichita's swankiest neighborhoods.

Jessica had made certain her daughter, Jo, was raised in a normal and stable home. There were riding lessons, piano lessons, but there was also a loving mother, who doted on her only child...her daughter.

Looking back, Jo should have recognized the signs of abuse...her mother's occasional black eye, the dark, purple bruises on her arms, the harsh words between her parents.

More than once, Jo questioned her mother about the injuries. Jessica would always brush them off, blaming herself for being clumsy...she'd bumped her head, ran into the corner of the closet door.

As Jo got older, during her teenage years, she heard the arguments...her father's long business trips out of town while Jessica and her daughter remained at home. She began to piece together the abuse and neglect Jessica had suffered at the hands of her rich and powerful husband...Jo's father.

Jo finished college, found a job a couple of hours from Wichita and rented a place of her own. Not long after moving away, she decided to leave work early one Friday and drive home to surprise her parents. And boy - what a surprise.

Jo went as far as to park on the street, and then walked down the drive, past her father's luxury sedan. She remembered unlocking the back door with her key, calling out her father's name as she dropped her purse and overnight bag on the kitchen table.

When her father didn't answer, she called out for Doria, their live-in housekeeper. Still no answer.

Jo wandered from the kitchen, through the butler's pantry and into the hall. The library door was ajar, and she could hear the sound of a woman's laughter on the other side.

"Dad?" Jo tentatively pushed the door open, onto the scene of her father cozied up on the settee with a woman Jo didn't recognize, wine glasses in their hands.

When Jo's father saw her standing in the doorway, he scrambled to his feet. The woman, unfazed by the interruption, let out a sultry laugh. "Andy, were you expecting company?"

Carlton shot the woman a quick glance. "You need to leave, Nicky."

Jo quickly recovered from her shock...all of the years of witnessing her mother's injuries at the hands of her father. A fury filled Jo like she'd never felt before. Her hate-filled eyes turned on him accusingly. "Don't bother. I was just leaving."

She slammed the door behind her and ran down the hall. Her father ran after her. "Jo! Joanna, come back here. I can explain."

Jo grabbed her things. She raced out of the house and down the long driveway. She didn't slow until she reached her car where she jumped inside and tore out of there.

She vaguely remembered driving out of their neighborhood and stopping at a nearby gas station. Her breaths came in short gasps with the image of her father and the other woman cozying up together burned in her mind.

Her fingers trembled as she dialed her mother's cell phone.

"Hello, Jo."

"Mom, I'm here."

"Here?"

"I just left the house." Jo's words tumbled out as she told her mother what she'd discovered.

Jessica Carlton was surprisingly calm. "I'm sorry you had to see that, Joanna. I never meant for him to hurt you."

"Hurt me?" Jo cried. "What about you? What about all of those years...the unexplained black eyes, the purple bruises, the limps. Dad hit you. You should've left."

Jessica cut her off. "I love you, Joanna, but you don't understand. It's not that easy to simply walk away."

"I'm going back to the house, but he needs to leave."

"I was on my way to an out-of-town meeting, but I'm turning around. I'm on my way home." Jessica promised to call her daughter when she reached Wichita.

Jo drove aimlessly before finally stopping at a nearby coffee shop, one she and her mother frequented. She sat staring sightlessly out the coffee shop window, and never gave it a second thought when she noticed several police cars and ambulances rush past. They turned into the gated neighborhood where Jo's parents lived.

She waited an agonizing hour, and as each minute passed, Jo grew more concerned for her mother's safety. She couldn't stand it any longer and finally called her mother.

Jessica's voice was calm. "I'm at the house, Joanna. The police are here."

"The police?"

"I'll explain when you get here."

When Jo arrived back at the house, she found patrol cars in the driveway, and a local television news van parked out front.

Something was terribly wrong. Jo pulled in behind the news van and raced up the driveway. An officer stopped her near the front walkway.

"My mother...my parents are inside. I'm Joanna Carlton."

"I'm sorry. I can't let you go in." The officer lifted his radio. "Joanna Carlton, the daughter, is here."

Jo stood next to the officer, waiting for her mother when a news reporter eased in next to her. He lifted his microphone and turned to face the camera. "We still have no word on the cause of death of local businessman, Andrew Carlton. I'm here now with a family member."

Jo's eyes grew wide, a horrified expression on her face. She was sure she had heard him wrong. Her father had been alive only a short time ago.

"Joanna." Jo spun around to find her mother facing her, handcuffed and accompanied by an officer. "I'm sorry, dear."

"The...reporter said Dad is dead." Jo searched her mother's face seeking some sort of confirmation that he was wrong.

"Yes." A small welt was beginning to form on the side of Jessica's cheek, and it dawned on Jo. The realization Jessica Carlton had finally had enough - had finally defended herself against the man who had abused her for decades.

"You..."

"I couldn't stand the thought that I worked so hard to shield you from the abuse, from the lies and your father's double life. He threw it all away on women who meant nothing...*nothing* to him."

"I'm sorry, Jo." Tears streamed down Jessica's face. "I love you, and I only wanted to protect you."

"But Dad...he hit you." Desperate to help her mother, Jo turned a pleading face to the officer. "My father abused my mother. He hit her. I'll testify to that. He physically and emotionally abused my mother for as long as I can remember."

"We need to go." The officer could see Jo was coming completely unglued and led Jessica away. Jo tried to follow after, but the other officer stopped her.

The rest of the day...the weeks and the months turned into a blur. Jo's mother was charged with her husband's death.

Jessica's attorneys worked hard to try to convince the jury she acted in self-defense. Jo took the stand in her mother's defense, sobbing unashamedly as she described the years of abuse her mother suffered at her father's hand.

In the end, Andrew Carlton, even in death, was able to abuse his wife one more time. The jury convicted Jessica Holden Carlton, and she was sentenced to live out the rest of her years inside the *Central State Women's Penitentiary*.

Jo visited her mother every Friday like clockwork. She spent every extra penny she earned at her marketing job on appeals, but it was all in vain. In the end, Jessica died less than a decade after her sentencing in her bunk and in her cell, clutching a faded photo of her daughter and her.

It took years of counseling for Jo to work through her grief and guilt over her parents' deaths. If only she hadn't walked in on her father. If only she hadn't called her mother. If only her mother hadn't confronted him. If only...

Jo slowly and painfully started to put the pieces of her life back together when an attorney showed up on her doorstep. With the death of both parents, the bulk of Andrew and Jessica Carlton's estate went to their only living relative...their daughter.

Gabe, Jo's husband, was long gone before she learned of the massive wealth.

She was shocked when the attorney explained that because of the nature of Jessica's incarceration and crime, the assets remained in limbo until her death. The attorney laid out the vast amount of assets in the financial portfolio, which also shocked Jo.

The local press went wild with the story...first with Jessica's death, dredging up the whole sordid story and then someone leaked Joanna's newfound wealth to the press. It got so bad; she refused to touch the money. She left it sitting in the accounts, moved to New York and tried to live her life as normally as possible.

Until the day...she ran across an ad for a house scheduled to be auctioned in the small town of Divine, Kansas, which was how Jo got to where she was today.

Delta dropped the weapon. She hit her knees and wrapped both arms around Jo. "Now, it's gonna be okay, Jo. He's just talking smack. He probably found you on the internet and concocted a plan to get his hands on your money."

"If he comes back, I'm going to pay him to go away." Jo began trembling violently. "I'll pay him off."

"No, you're not, because once he gets money from you, hc'll come back again and again. He'll never leave you alone. You heard him. He already has it in his mind he wants the farm."

"I can't let that happen. The women, you, Nash, Gary...this is my home." Jo could feel hysteria starting to set in. "What am I going to do?"

"We'll figure it out," Delta said. "I can guarantee you one thing for certain...we're not going to let that man railroad you. We're not going down without a fight."

Chapter 8

Delta gave Jo a hand up and released her grip once her friend was on her feet. "The first thing we're going to do is get ahold of one of those high-powered attorneys you have on retainer, do a little digging around and find out more about this investigator, Neil Garland, and Parker."

"You're right. We should start there. The investigator's business card is on my desk."

The women stepped back inside the kitchen and Jo made a beeline for her office. She returned with the card and her cell phone in hand.

She waited for Delta to join her at the kitchen table.

Jo scrolled through the contact list, bypassing her attorney's personal cell phone number and dialing the law firm instead. "I trust Chris Nyles. He was the attorney I used for my mother's trial and the one who helped me navigate the legal mumbo jumbo when I purchased this property."

"Your mother still ended up in prison," Delta said.

"It wasn't Chris's fault. My father had too many connections...too many people, including powerful members of the press, who convicted my mother before her case ever went to trial."

Jo held up a finger as the call rang through.

"Nyles and Hartman. How can I help you?"

"Yes, this is Joanna Pepperdine. I would like to leave a message for Chris Nyles please."

"Hold one moment." The line went silent as Jo waited.

"Joanna Pepperdine." Chris's booming voice echoed through the phone. "I was just thinking about you the other day. How is life down on the farm - or should I say up on the farm?"

"Charming, exciting, exhausting, everything I expected." Jo smiled. Chris had not only been her legal adviser for the purchase of the farm, but she'd also leaned on him heavily for support during her mother's long drawn out and very public trial.

Chris was there at all hours for Jo, during the darkest moments, the darkest period in her life. Even after Jessica Carlton's conviction and incarceration, Chris kept in touch with her.

He was more like family than a business associate, and she trusted him implicitly. "I love the farm. The halfway house is working out better than I ever imagined." She shot Delta a quick look.

"I made some wonderful friends and even hired one of them. As fate would have it, Delta, my right-hand gal, was a prison cook at *Central* before I hired her to help me run my businesses and run the house."

"I need to stop by one of these days when I'm on my way to Kansas City."

"Chris, you and I both know Divine is not on the way to Kansas City."

"Then I'll make a day of it. We'll have lunch."

"I would love to see you," Jo sobered. "I'm sorry to bother you, but I need help." She briefly explained how the private investigator showed up at the farm to track her down, hinting at a long-lost relative. "This morning, a man by the name of Miles Parker showed up on my doorstep. He claims he's my half-brother, that his mother and my father were having an affair."

"And he's coming forward after all this time?"

"He said he found out about his real father and me when he was going through his mother's things after she died. He claims he never knew who his father was until then."

There was a moment of silence on the other end and then Chris cleared his throat, a sign he was perturbed. "What do you think, Jo? Is it possible this man is your half-brother?"

Jo began to pace. "Yesterday, I would have said no way, not possible, but you know the circumstances. My father was no saint. Is it possible? My heart tells me 'no,' but my gut is going in a different direction."

"I see. Tell me everything you know...names, locations, the private investigator's name. I'll do a little digging around."

Jo rattled off the private investigator's information first. "Miles Parker is the name of the man claiming to be my half-brother. His mother's name was Irene Parker, a woman who supposedly worked for my father in Wichita. After she became pregnant, Parker claims Dad sent them off to California, but he continued to send checks to support them until Parker turned eighteen."

"This is a good start. Do you have any idea how old Miles Parker may be? Just a ballpark guesstimate would help."

Jo glanced at Delta. "How old do you think Miles Parker is?"

"Early forties."

"That would be my guess." Jo shifted the phone closer to her face. "I would guess he's in his early forties."

"I'll start digging around today," Chris promised. "The investigator's name sounds vaguely familiar. It will be easy for me to get information on him. I could call in a few favors and find out pretty quickly if this claim has any potential to be legit."

Jo was already beginning to feel better, knowing someone with more experience in these matters, not to mention legal background, was going to help her. "Thank you, Chris. Just send me your bill."

"I'm not going to charge you, Jo. This is a favor for a friend."

"That's not fair to you."

"Tell you what...when I get to Divine, you can take me out to lunch."

"It's a deal." Jo thanked him again before disconnecting the call. "Chris is going to look into it."

"Perfect." Delta patted Jo's shoulder. "In the meantime, you need to put this whole thing out of your mind. There's nothing you can do and no sense in worrying about something that may be nothing."

Although Delta was right, Jo was frightened to death. What if what Miles Parker said was true and he was her half-brother? Would he have a legitimate claim to Jo's fortune...or worse yet, a claim to her beloved *Second Chance* farm?

More than anything, Jo wanted to believe the man was an opportunist, someone who found out about Jo's history and saw an opportunity to make a quick buck. She still wasn't ruling out paying the man off to make him go away.

Surely, there was some sort of ironclad legal agreement Chris could draw up where the man would forfeit any rights in exchange for cash.

The next couple of hours passed in a blur with Jo darting from the mercantile to the bakeshop to Nash's workshop. It was almost time to pick Sherry up at the deli, with a few minutes to spare to swing by *Four Corners Mini-Mart* on her way.

There was no one at the pumps and only one car in the parking lot when Jo arrived. She went inside and then wandered the aisles, searching for something to purchase.

She settled on a bag of chips and then carried it to the counter where a young man stood waiting.

"This is it?" The man eyed the chips.

"Yes. Is there a minimum for purchases?" Jo joked.

"No, but it's buy one, get one free."

"Whoops." Jo returned to the rack and grabbed another bag of chips before returning to the counter. She pulled a ten from her wallet and handed it to him. "I'm sorry to hear about your co-worker, Janet's death."

"It is pretty sad. She was already on her way out."

Jo watched the man count out her change. "On her way out?"

"She was quitting. She put in her notice. For some reason, she freaked out. I wasn't here, but that's what I heard."

"I see." Jo thanked the man as she placed her change inside her purse and gave him a quick smile before exiting the store.

It was a short drive from the gas station to the deli. Since it was in between the lunch and dinner crowd, there weren't many diners inside.

Jo found Sherry in the back, talking to Marlee and a couple of the other employees. "How was work?"

"Okay." Sherry wrinkled her nose.

"Busy." Marlee ran a ragged hand through her hair. "This place was a madhouse. We hosted a *Divine Fall Festival* committee meeting, followed by a town hall meeting for residents to add their input."

"You had it here?"

"Yeah. Mrs. White, the local librarian who was in charge of the meeting, asked if they could hold it here. I figured a dozen or so people would show up."

"It was wall-to-wall people," Sherry said. "On the bright side, I made quite a bit in tips."

"Yes, you did." Marlee smiled gratefully. "Thank you so much for all of your hard work."

"You're welcome. I met some nice locals."

"Except for one old crabapple."

"Who gave Sherry a hard time," Jo guessed.

"She refused to allow Sherry to serve her."

"It's okay," Sherry said. "I understand. People are sometimes scared of ex-cons like me, even if they don't know the circumstances."

"You may understand, but it doesn't make it right." Marlee changed the subject. "I was surprised no one asked about Janet's death."

"They did, I mean a couple of people did," Sherry said. "I guess she was fairly new to the area."

"Fairly new if you consider living here for a year new to the area. Her boyfriend isn't." Marlee explained Janet had moved in with her boyfriend, Owen, who was a local. His family had lived in the area for as long as Marlee could remember. "Owen, along with his parents and siblings, lives in a compound of mobile homes out past the sheriff's department."

"I stopped by the gas station/mini-mart on my way here and found out something interesting." Jo told them about her conversation with the station clerk, how Janet had put in her notice.

Marlee frowned. "You're serious? She told me she wasn't quitting her other job, that she needed the money. I wonder if she had another job lined up and was lying to me."

One of the servers hurried into the back. "Marlee, I'm sorry to bother you, but one of the guests is complaining about her eggs benedict. She said there's no meat on it."

"Oh no," Marlee groaned. "Not again. I swear I'm losing my mind."

"We'll get out of your hair." Jo, along with Sherry, followed Marlee into the dining room.

"See you tomorrow morning," Sherry told Marlee on her way past.

"You betcha."

Jo waited until they were on the road to talk. "Are you still enjoying your job at the deli?"

"Oh yes." Sherry nodded enthusiastically. "The time flies by."

She grew quiet as she stared out the window. "It's probably a good thing not everyone is nice. I need to learn to deal with it. My past is going to haunt me wherever I go. There will be people who won't like

108

me, people who won't trust me, people who won't hire me. Marlee hiring me is another step toward me getting back on my feet and on my own."

"You're right." Jo cast the woman a sideways glance. Sherry was the "senior" resident, meaning she'd been with Jo the longest.

Not only had she been incarcerated at the women's prison, but according to what Sherry had shared with Jo, prior to her arrest she had been living on the streets and scrounging through garbage cans for food.

"Have you given any more thought to reaching out to your family?" Sherry had told Jo that she had family in Southern Nebraska. The last communication was a phone call right after Sherry's sentencing.

Sherry had called home, and her father had answered the phone. When she explained she needed help, her father hung up on her and she never tried to call again.

"I...a little." Sherry began picking at her fingernail.

"Time heals a lot of things," Jo said softly. "It's been years since you last called your family. Perhaps it's time to give it another try."

Sherry didn't speak and instead, silently nodded.

"You've come so far, Sherry. You're turning your life around. Just look at you. You have a job, you're learning new skills and you have good solid friends."

"I have you."

"Right," Jo smiled. "You won't know unless you try. We can make the call together. Do you still have the number?"

"Yeah." Sherry tapped the side of her head. "I have the telephone number memorized."

"When you're ready, you give me the word, and I'll loan you my cell phone. You can make the call in my office, where it's private."

Sherry grinned. "Okay. It's a deal."

Jo changed the subject, and they discussed the fall decorating party and the afternoon self-defense class. "I think Delta is starting to tweak her recipe for the upcoming baking contest. Has Marlee slipped on what she plans to make?"

"Nope. She's tight-lipped about the entire thing. I think she suspects I'm spying on her and reporting back to Delta. I don't want to be caught in the middle of the competition."

"And neither do I. I love them both dearly and wish them the best," Jo said. "Maybe it will end in a tie. Delta's making...."

Sherry lifted a hand. "No. Don't tell me. That way, if Marlee tries to pump me for information, I can honestly tell her I don't know."

Jo chuckled. "You're right. Okay. My lips are sealed."

They reached the farm, and Sherry followed Jo to the front of the vehicle.

"Is there something else?"

"About that call…maybe it is time to try again," Sherry said.

"Whenever you're ready, you let me know." Jo waited until Sherry strolled across the gravel drive and disappeared behind the buildings.

She found Delta in the kitchen, surrounded by pumpkins. "What're you doing?"

"I'm getting the pumpkins prepped for carving." Delta scooped out a handful of pumpkin seeds and set them on a plate. "Any word on Marlee's recipe?"

"No, and I didn't ask. Sherry and I both agreed we don't want to get caught in the middle."

"That's not fair," Delta frowned.

"So you're willing to let Marlee know what you're working on?"

"No." Delta's frown deepened. "Whose side are you on?"

"I'm not on anyone's side. Actually, I'm on both of your sides." Jo leaned her hip against the counter. "I stopped by the gas station on my way to pick Sherry up. Janet Ferris had put in her notice. She was quitting her job at the gas station."

"To work full-time for Marlee?"

"Nope."

"So why was she quitting?" Delta asked.

"Good question and another valid question is why did the woman freak out? It seems she may have been unstable in the hours leading up to her death."

"Definitely emotionally unstable," Delta agreed. "Does Sherry still like the job?"

"So far." Jo started to tell her about the conversation with Sherry when the back door opened and she stepped inside. "Are you working with Delta?"

"No." Sherry tugged on the corner of her blouse. "I thought about what you said, and I'm ready."

"You're ready to reach out to your family?"

"Yes. If you have time. If you're busy, we can do it another time."

"Now is good." Jo gently led Sherry through the kitchen and into her office. "We can make the call in here."

Jo closed the door behind them and waited for Sherry to have a seat before settling in behind the desk. She unplugged her cell phone from the charger and handed it to Sherry. "Before we place the call, let's talk."

"Okay."

"It's been years since you've had any communication with your family."

"Yes." Sherry nodded.

"The last time you called, your father found out it was you and he hung up."

"Yep." Sherry began spinning the cell phone in a small circle. "I told him I was in trouble and needed help. He never gave me a chance to explain before he hung up."

"So let's run through a couple of different scenarios," Jo said. "What if you reach him again and he hangs up?"

Sherry shrugged. "I wouldn't be surprised. I think my family wrote me off. They might even think I'm dead by now."

Jo's heart sank at the words. She would give anything to have a family, her family still alive - her mother alive. "We need to prepare ourselves for the chance that's exactly what will happen."

"Right."

"Are you sure you're ready? We don't have to do this."

Sherry continued spinning the phone...around and around while Jo silently watched her. She could see the inner turmoil, how apprehensive she was about possibly facing another rejection by her family.

"I..." Sherry abruptly stood and then just as abruptly sat again. "I put my family through a lot, but I'm a changed person. The old Sherry, the one they knew, she's gone."

"You're right. The old Sherry is gone."

Sherry's eyes met Jo's eyes, and she sucked in a breath. "I'm ready to make the call."

Chapter 9

Sherry's fingers trembled as she tapped the phone screen. "You would think after all of this time I would have forgotten the number." Her face turned a shade of ghostly white. "It's ringing...it went to voice mail. That's my dad's voice," she told Jo excitedly.

There was a tremor in her voice as she left a brief message. "Hello, Dad. It's me...Sherry. I...I wanted to let you know..." She shot Jo a terrified look, and Jo nodded encouragingly.

"I was released from prison. I straightened my life out. I have a job now, and I'm living on a farm near Divine, Kansas. It's a couple of hours west of Kansas City. I...I'm sorry for what happened in the past, for hurting you and Mom and the family, and I was hoping to talk to you. You can call me back or better yet, I'll try back again, maybe later..." Her sentence trailed off, and she ended the message with a hasty "good-bye."

Sherry disconnected the call and handed the phone to Jo. "How did I do?"

"You did great...wonderful. You said just enough, that you were on the right track, you had a job."

"Now what?"

"We can try again later today or tomorrow,"

Sherry nodded nervously. "Right. Maybe we can try again later." She stood. "I better get going. I have to cover my shift in the mercantile."

Jo followed her out of the house and to the front porch.

Sherry grasped the handrail and started down the steps before turning back. "Thanks, Jo."

"You're welcome. I'm proud of you, Sherry. Every day is a step in the right direction, a day closer to a wonderful and exciting new life."

"You're right. I'm proud of me, too." Sherry straightened her shoulders and marched across the driveway while Jo offered up a small prayer for her. Would the family welcome her back with open arms? Or would she face another heart-wrenching rejection?

For Sherry's sake, Jo hoped this was the beginning of healing with the family. If not, Jo and the others, her other family, would be there for her. Sometimes family wasn't the ones you were born with, but the ones you grew to love, the ones you counted on to support you, the ones who had your back when the going got tough.

She slowly made her way back inside.

Delta stood at the kitchen counter crushing cookies in a large bowl. Jo attempted to take a sneak peek inside.

"Uh...uh...uh." Delta folded her arms, blocking Jo's view of the bowl's contents. "No peeking."

"Fine." Jo shoved a hand on her hip. "If you're going to keep the recipe top secret, how do you plan on finding volunteer taste-testers?"

"Oh, you can taste-test all right, but I can't let you see the ingredients. I may have to blindfold you. But first, you gotta get out of my kitchen." Delta shooed Jo away, so she headed to Nash's workshop to chat.

Nash was working alongside Kelli, one of the other residents. "Hey, Jo." A smile lit his face. "What brings you to my neck of the woods?"

"Delta kicked me out of the kitchen. I think she's working on her super-secret recipe for the fall baking contest. What are you making?"

"Remember me mentioning a fall decoration? Check it out." Nash stepped to the side, revealing a large wooden barrel, the outline of a jack-o-lantern face carved on the front. "I'm making a set of three. I figured we could put them on the porch, between the entrance to the mercantile and the bakeshop."

"How clever." Jo ran her finger along the pumpkin's tooth. "We could put some large battery candles inside."

"That's not all." Kelli patted the top. "Nash put a sealer on the outside. We're going to turn the top into a candy dish, so shoppers can help themselves to a piece of candy or a special treat on their way in."

"And I know just the place to get all of the hard candy we'll need." Jo had recently discovered that *Tool Time*, Divine's hardware store, stocked large barrels of hard candy. "I love it."

"Thanks," Nash said.

"Thank you for making such fun decorations." Jo glanced at her watch. "I better go change. I wanted to remind you of our self-defense class at five."

"Right." Nash nodded. "I'm covering the mercantile and Claire from the antique shop is going to watch the bakeshop."

121

"Yes. The class is only an hour long. Thanks again for offering to help." Jo stepped out of Nash's workshop, heading back toward the house when a vehicle pulled into the drive.

It was a Smith County police vehicle. Deputy Brian Franklin climbed out of the car and met Jo in front of the bakeshop.

"Hello, Jo."

"Good afternoon, Deputy Franklin. Are you here to buy some donuts?" she teased.

"No. I wish. I was wondering if I could have a word with one of your residents." The deputy pulled a notepad from his pocket and flipped it open. "Sherry Marshall. She works part-time at *Divine Delicatessen*."

"Is this about Janet Ferris' death?"

"Murder." The deputy nodded. "I'm helping with the investigation, and I want to ask her a few questions."

"Of course." Jo held up a finger. "I'll go track her down." She made a quick pass through the mercantile and bakeshop, but Sherry wasn't there.

She found the woman in the common area, washing dishes in the sink.

"Hey." Sherry did a double take. "Did my family call back?"

"No. Not yet. Deputy Franklin is here. He would like to ask you a few questions about Janet."

"Oh." Sherry's face fell.

"Don't worry. I'll be right there with you." Jo led Sherry out of the room to where the deputy was waiting.

Franklin tipped his hat. "I'm sorry to bother you, Ms. Marshall. I'm helping with the investigation into Janet Ferris' death and wanted to ask you a few questions."

"Of course."

Franklin started by asking general questions, how long Sherry had known Ferris, if they had any contact outside of work, if there had been any disagreements between them.

"Yes. Janet didn't like me. I think she resented having to train me."

"Did you argue with Ms. Ferris the day of her death?"

Sherry shot Jo a quick glance before answering. "Yes. As I said, she wasn't keen on having to train me. She was getting in my face. She was also using her cell phone during working hours. I got fed up and told her I was going to report her."

"Did you see her again after that...perhaps while you were on break?"

"I object," Jo said.

The deputy paused, pen in hand. "This isn't a court case. I'm merely asking if there was additional interaction after the original altercation."

"You're leading Sherry. We both know Ferris' body was found inside her car, parked out behind the deli."

"Then let me pose the question differently…did you take a break?"

"I did." Sherry nodded. "I walked to the bank down the street to make a deposit. On the way back, I stopped at the *Twistee Treat* before returning to work. I have a time-stamped bank receipt."

"What about your stop at *Twistee Treat*? Do you have a receipt?"

"No. I paid in cash," Sherry said.

"So we can't verify your whereabouts for part of your break." The deputy scribbled furiously.

"I ordered a fruit smoothie. The woman who waited on me was older, with grayish hair, pulled back in a bun. She may remember me because she recognized the deli uniform and asked me if I worked for Marlee."

"That's helpful. I appreciate the information. Is there anything else you would like to tell me, something you may have forgotten?"

"No."

The women were silent while the deputy continued writing. He flipped the notepad shut and tucked that, along with the pen, in his front pocket.

"Surely, you're talking to the mini-mart employees," Jo said. "Rumor has it Janet made a scene at the gas station during her break, right before her death."

"Yes, we're questioning the station employees, as well."

"But you have no suspects yet?"

"We have a few." The deputy tilted his head. "Are you certain you only had one run-in with Ms. Ferris?"

"Positive," Sherry said. "Why do you keep asking?"

"Because Ferris' boyfriend, Owen Cole, claims she was deathly afraid of you and even hinted you were threatening her."

Sherry's jaw dropped. "That's crazy. I never threatened the woman, unless telling her I was going to report her for using her cell phone during working hours is considered a threat."

"That's all I have for now." The deputy thanked Sherry for her time before climbing into his patrol car and driving off.

"I get a bad feeling about this," Jo said. "Something isn't adding up. It sounds as if Janet Ferris was emotionally unstable. She went on some sort of rampage after you two argued."

"And she was lying," Sherry said. "We had one small argument. She didn't like training me. Maybe she was afraid of me, like others who have a pre-conceived notion that every single person who has been incarcerated is a lifetime criminal. Once a criminal, always a criminal."

Jo sighed heavily. She was right. The fact the woman told others she was afraid of Sherry was unsettling. The women arguing before Janet's death was another strike against her.

"Hopefully, the deputy will follow up with the ice cream shop and corroborate your story."

"Or maybe he won't bother. I better get to work."

"Don't forget our five o'clock self-defense class in the barn."

"I won't." Sherry made her way into the mercantile while Jo returned to the house. She stepped inside to an aroma she could only describe as Christmas in the south, a combination of fried chicken and cinnamon.

She made it as far as the kitchen where she caught a glimpse of Delta darting back and forth. Leah, Delta's current assistant, hovered off to the side.

Delta muttered under her breath as she banged a pan on the counter.

Jo backed out of the kitchen, anxious to steer clear of the kitchen and suspecting that her friend's latest round of test recipes weren't turning out as planned.

She returned to her office and began sorting through her emails. Jo's attorney had promised to contact her as soon as he had information about Miles Parker's claim of being related, but so far, there was no email from her friend.

She began working on the important task of updating the residents' files. From day one, Jo had kept files on each of the women to help track their progress. She checked off the boxes for the life skills section when the women learned how to open and balance a checking account.

In addition to opening and balancing the accounts, the women learned how to fill out job applications, submit resumes; there was also a driver's refresher course. She even went over filling out a rental application, and the list went on.

Sherry had made the most progress. Now that she'd found a job and was learning new skills, Jo knew it would only be a matter of time before the woman would be ready to venture out on her own.

Jo finished typing some notes in each of the women's files and then exited out of the screen. She noticed her cell phone, sitting on the corner of the desk. There was one missed call. She entered the password and pressed the message key.

"Yes, this is Ben Marshall. This message is for Sherry Marshall. Please inform Ms. Marshall the family wishes no contact from her. The daughter we once knew is dead."

Chapter 10

Jo waited for more, but that was the end of the message. She listened to it twice, just to make sure she hadn't missed anything.

"What's wrong?" Delta stood in the doorway. "You look like you lost your best friend."

"Sherry's father left a message on my cell phone."

"Uh-oh." Delta plopped down in the chair. "It wasn't good."

"Nope. He told me the family wants no contact from Sherry and they consider her dead."

Delta's hand flew to her mouth. "They aren't even going to give her a chance? Did she tell them she has a job and that she's turned her life around?"

"Yes, but it appears it doesn't matter." Jo shifted her gaze, staring sightlessly out the window. "This is my fault. I encouraged her to make the call."

"I don't understand how you can turn your back on family. Whatever happened to giving a loved one a second chance?"

"Apparently, for whatever reason, they wrote her off."

"How are you going to tell her?" Delta asked.

"I don't know." Jo slowly turned, her eyes locking with Delta's eyes. "This will be a terrible blow. First, we have the woman's death at the deli and now this."

"Well, certainly the authorities don't believe Sherry had anything to do with Janet's death."

"Deputy Franklin stopped by here a short time ago. Apparently, Ms. Ferris confided to her boyfriend she was afraid of Sherry. Sherry admitted they argued and now the woman is dead."

"The woman was troubled." Delta twirled her finger in a circular motion near her forehead. "I talked to my niece, Patti, earlier. She claims Janet was totally off her rocker."

"It is what it is." Jo's shoulders drooped. "I guess I better head over to the barn. Our self-defense class is starting in a few minutes."

"Now this I gotta see." Delta followed Jo out of the office. She went to get Leah, who was drying dishes, and then the women made their way to the barn.

Duke, Jo's hound, caught up with them and trotted ahead. They were halfway there when Claire's car pulled into the drive.

Claire, along with a man who appeared to be around Jo's age, exited the car. They met the trio near the back. "Hello, Jo. We made it right on time."

"Yes, you did. Thank you for coming. This means a lot to me...to us."

"You're welcome." Claire turned to the man. "This is my nephew, Mark. Mark, this is Joanna Pepperdine."

The man smiled as he reached for Jo's hand. "Nice to meet you."

"And I already know this young lady." Mark shook Delta's hand next.

"Flattery will get you everywhere."

He shook Leah's hand while Claire finished the introductions.

"We're holding the self-defense class in the barn," Jo explained. "It's the only place with enough room."

"I'll take over in the bakeshop and send the gals your way." Claire hurried inside while the women and Mark walked to the barn.

After everyone had assembled, Jo introduced Claire's nephew to the women.

"Welcome. My name is Mark. I'm a former Kansas Highway Patrol officer. Joanna invited me to come here this afternoon to talk about safety and also demonstrate a few self-defense moves." The former officer reminded the women to be aware of their surroundings at all times, to listen to their gut and to be watchful of others.

"Now that I've gone over a few safety tips, I would like to demonstrate some basic safety maneuvers. I'm going to need a volunteer."

All of the women's hands shot up, except for Michelle and Jo.

"I'll take you." The man pointed to Kelli, who promptly popped out of her chair and crossed to the front. "The first move involves using your forearm to strike your attacker in the throat."

He showed Kelli how to lift her arm, using her forearm and body's momentum to strike him in the throat and knock him off balance.

"This is the first stage of the self-defense move. Now that I'm off balance, Kelli will deliver the next blow - a strike to my midsection, to my solar plexus using her elbow."

Mark aligned Kelli's elbow with her shoulder and slowly moved her forward, using momentum to jab her elbow into his midsection.

"Good...good," he said. "Excellent and now a final move. You've chopped me, your attacker, in the throat, and used your elbow to jab my midsection. I'm halfway down. What's your next move?"

"A knee to the groin," Kelli guessed.

"Bingo."

Kelli performed a slow knee to the groin movement to demonstrate.

"You've got it." Mark lifted a finger. "Just remember these three...chop, jab and knee."

"Chop, jab and knee." Kelli batted her eyes at the attractive instructor. "You can teach me a thing or two anytime."

"I...uh," Mark stuttered. "Thank you, Kelli."

Kelli offered him a dazzling smile and reluctantly returned to her seat while Mark continued talking about safety, including how to stay safe at ATMs, while pumping gas and even walking to the car.

After they finished, Delta, who stood silently in the back watching, clapped her hands and the others joined her. "I learned a thing or two myself. I have a jug of apple cider in the bakeshop, along with a new recipe I'm testing out and of course, some pumpkin spice cookies."

The women filed out of the barn. Jo stood near the door and waited for Mark. "Thank you so much for coming here. How much do I owe you for your time?"

"I'll take cookies and cider for pay," Mark joked.

"No, seriously," Jo said. "I didn't expect you to work for free."

"I consider this my small contribution to the work you're doing. Aunt Claire told me all about this place. Having worked in law enforcement, I know the drill. You're giving these women a second chance, something so many more need but will never get."

"Then please accept my sincere gratitude for your volunteer work." Jo was curious. "You're young...so why did you get out of law enforcement?"

"I was injured on the job, shot in the back during a traffic stop. I had to have a few parts fused together, making it impossible for me to pursue on foot. I officially retired and started offering self-defense classes. I also offer gun safety and concealed weapons permit classes if you're interested."

"Not for the women," Jo said. "Delta is a bit of a weapons expert. The women here...they can't buy guns, but I appreciate the offer."

Mark waited for Jo to slide the barn door shut. "Delta...she's a trip. She used to run the women's prison kitchen with an iron fist."

"She runs this place with an iron rolling pin, but I can't imagine life without her."

Mark and Jo began strolling toward the mercantile. "So what's your story? What possessed a single woman to open a halfway house for former convicts?"

"If I told you, I would have to kill you," Jo joked.

"Ah, so it's a secret."

"Not really a secret. A family member was incarcerated. I did everything I could to help free her." Jo sobered. "She died in prison before getting her second chance. It took me a while, but I finally figured out what God wanted me to do. He gave me this very special place, and here I am."

"It sounds like the makings of a movie."

"Not for me," Jo laughed. "I prefer to fly under the radar."

Nash, Claire, the women, along with Delta were already inside.

Jo waited for Mark to grab some goodies and then approached the counter where Delta was dishing out the food. "Are any of these a contender for the contest?"

"Yes. It's my raspberry dream bars." Delta eased a raspberry bar onto a small paper plate and handed it to Jo, who promptly sniffed the top. "It smells good." She lifted the plate. "It has a layer of cream cheese with a different crust."

"Take a bite." Delta watched as Jo nibbled the corner.

She detected a hint of cream cheese, along with the raspberries and a crumble topping. "What's in the crust? It's not graham cracker."

"The crust is crushed vanilla wafers and pecans, followed by a layer of cream cheese and raspberry jam. It's topped with a combination of brown sugar, cinnamon and oatmeal. Do you like it?"

Jo took another bite. She closed her eyes, savoring the rich, crunchy flavors. "Yes...this most definitely needs to be a contender for the contest."

After getting Jo's feedback, Delta made her rounds asking for the others' opinions and everyone agreed she had a winner.

Claire and Mark were the first to leave, with Jo thanking both of them again for taking the time to come by.

The other women began heading to the house to help Delta set the dinner table.

Sherry hung back to help Jo tidy the bakeshop. She waited for her to finish locking up. "I was wondering if you heard back...if you got a message."

Jo's heart skipped a beat. She'd hoped to have time to think of her response, how she could break the news to Sherry without upsetting her, but it was too late. "I...yes, Sherry, I did get a call back."

"From my dad?"

"Yes, your father called."

"What did he say?"

Chapter 11

Jo hesitated as she searched for the right words. "Let's go sit on the porch." She linked arms with Sherry, and they began strolling across the drive.

Everyone else had gone ahead except for Nash. He locked the workshop door and caught up with them. "How was the self-defense class?"

"It was good," Jo said. "Mark did a great job of going over some basic safety information and a few self-defense moves. It was well worth the time and effort."

"Yes, it was," Sherry agreed. "Plus, he was cute, which was a bonus."

"Cute?" Nash lifted a brow and gazed at Jo, who smiled innocently. "Did I say he was cute? He was nice."

They reached the front porch, and Jo paused to greet Duke, who stood waiting at the bottom of the steps. "Sherry and I are going to hang out here for a few minutes."

Nash gave Jo a questioning look but didn't comment. Instead, he nodded. "I'll see you inside."

Jo wandered over to the swing and sat down. She patted the seat next to her. "This spot has your name all over it."

Sherry gingerly perched on the edge of the swing, her back ramrod straight and an unreadable expression on her face. "The message...it wasn't what I hoped."

"No." Jo sucked in a breath and studied the woman's face. "I'm sorry, Sherry. I'm sorry I encouraged you to call your family. I just thought..."

"You can't blame yourself, Jo. You gave me a choice. You didn't force me to make the call." Sherry laughed bitterly. "Imagine that you - a complete stranger - would open your home to me, you would treat me like family but my own family, my own flesh and blood can't find it in their hearts to do the same."

"I don't know what to say," Jo briefly closed her eyes, praying God would give her the right words to heal the wounds. "I don't know your whole history, what happened in your past. You asked for your father's forgiveness. You extended the olive branch, and now it's up to him...to them to make the next move."

"Right." A tear trailed down Sherry's cheek. "I wanted a second chance, a chance to prove to them that I've changed." She turned to Jo, her tear-filled eyes haunted. "Do you think they might reconsider?"

"Maybe." Jo reached for Sherry's hand. "We can pray for God to work on the situation. The important thing is you're seeking forgiveness. You're willing to mend those relationships, and that's a big step."

"It is." Although Sherry said the words, Jo could see she was still hurting.

"You must also forgive yourself," Jo said softly. "The past is over. This is your new start. You're a different person now."

"I am," Sherry whispered.

"You opened the door. You made the first move. You were very brave to do that, to open yourself up to rejection. No matter what happens, we love you. All of us...Delta, Nash, Gary, Raylene and the other women."

"You're right," Sherry said. "Maybe they need more time. I took my dad by surprise."

"So we're not going to dwell on his initial reaction. I'm proud of you, and you need to be proud of you, too. This is the first step. I say we leave it in God's hands," Jo said. "Would you like to pray about it?"

"Yeah."

The women bowed their heads, and Jo began to pray.

"Dear Heavenly Father, we come before you today and pray for Sherry. Lord, you know her past; you know how hard she's working to turn her life around, to make amends to those she loves. We pray for forgiveness in the hearts of all involved, that you bring healing into all of their lives."

She continued. "Thank you for bringing Sherry to us, for allowing her to become a part of our family now and forever, no matter what happens. We pray for peace for Sherry. Wrap her in your loving arms in her time of hurt. Thank you, God, for your Son, our Savior Jesus. Amen."

Jo lifted her head and wiped the tears from her own eyes. "I have a Bible verse I want you to remember. In fact, I'm going to print it off and give you a copy when we go inside."

"Brothers and sisters, I do not consider myself yet to have taken hold of it. But one thing I do:

Forgetting what is behind and straining toward what is ahead..." Philippians 3:13 (NIV)

"The old Sherry is gone. The new one is looking ahead. Remember that."

Sherry looked as if she was about to say something, and Jo suspected she was going to ask what her father had said. It was a message Jo hoped she wouldn't have to repeat.

Delta saved the day when she swung the screen door open and stepped onto the porch. "There you are. Dinner is ready." She eyed Sherry and Jo's splotchy red faces. "Oh no. Every time I come out on this porch, someone is crying. I'm gonna have to leave a Kleenex cabinet out here. Is Jo making you cry? Cuz if she is, I'm gonna take her out back and give her a tongue-lashing."

Sherry pressed her fingers to her eyelids and giggled. "No. Jo didn't make me cry. She's trying to cheer me up."

"Good, cuz it's never a good idea to chew out the boss." Delta motioned them inside. "If you're done cryin' you better head inside before our hungry tribe eats all of the food."

Jo stepped inside while Delta flung her arm around Sherry's shoulders. "I made a batch of my finger lickin' fried chicken, some sour cream mashed potatoes and fresh-from-the-garden corn on the cob. I hope you're hungry."

"I'm starving," Sherry said.

The trio joined the others as they gathered around the dining room table. Jo smoothed her napkin in her lap and then asked Nash to pray.

After he finished, they dug in, gobbling up their food while Delta questioned, or more like interrogated them, about her raspberry bars.

"They were delightful," Jo said. "I think the bars are the perfect recipe for the baking contest."

The others chimed in, echoing Jo's sentiment. Still not convinced, Delta insisted it needed more tweaking.

Because they'd eaten sweet treats after the self-defense class, Delta skipped dessert and offered them coffee instead.

They chatted about the class, all unanimously agreeing they learned something new. After finishing the coffee, the women helped clean up while Jo ran to her office to print off the Bible verse.

When she returned to the kitchen, the only ones left were Sherry and Delta. Jo handed the paper to Sherry.

"Thanks, Jo. Thanks for everything." She quickly read it before folding the sheet in thirds and tucking it inside her pocket.

Jo glanced around the empty kitchen. "Where's the fire? Everyone was in a hurry to leave tonight."

"We're playing cards in the common area. Tara brought a deck with her and asked us if we wanted to play."

"That sounds like fun." A flicker of concern crossed Jo's face. "You're not playing for money, are you?"

"No," Sherry laughed. "We're playing for fun. Or maybe we could play for jobs."

Jo's curiosity was piqued. "Are some jobs more popular than others?" She'd never thought about it, but obviously, some of the women would prefer certain jobs over others, although they all paid the same.

"You could say that."

"What is the most coveted job?" Jo asked.

Sherry shifted her feet, looking slightly uncomfortable. "I...uh. Well, it's not necessarily *my* favorite job, but the women like to work in the workshop with Nash."

"Mmm. Hmm." Delta, who was putting the last of the leftovers in the fridge, wandered over. "And do you know *why* they like working with Nash?"

Sherry scratched the tip of her nose and averted her gaze.

"You don't have to answer," Delta said. "They want to work with Nash because he is one fine looking man."

"Maybe. I mean, like I said, it's not necessarily my favorite job, although I like working with Nash. I also like working in the gardens with Gary, being outdoors and enjoying the fresh air. I better get going." Sherry darted out the door before Delta could reply.

Jo pointed at her friend. "You put poor Sherry on the spot."

"I told you."

"Told me what?"

Delta batted her eyes. She clasped her hands and pretended to swoon. "The women are gaga over Nash, and he only has eyes for you."

"I wish you would stop saying that." Jo could feel her cheeks redden. "I'm his boss."

"If that's the only thing holding you back from admitting you're interested, then you should fire him so you can date."

Jo snorted. "Delta Childress, stop with your matchmaking."

"Fine. Someday, hopefully soon, you'll come to your senses, and I'll be right here ready to tell you I told you so."

"We'll see," Jo muttered.

Delta changed the subject. "You hear back from that fancy lawyer friend of yours yet?"

"No." Jo had almost forgotten about Miles Parker and Neil Garland, the private investigator. "I was thinking I might do a little digging around on my own while I wait."

Delta followed Jo into her office. "Social media is a great place to start."

"Right."

"I have some other ideas." Delta didn't wait for an invitation. She grabbed one of the chairs and dragged it behind the desk and close to Jo's chair. "Now, I know you trust this attorney and I'm sure he's trying to help, but I've been doing some thinking."

"And?"

"Even if the attorney tells you this Miles character is flesh and blood, we need to do our own due diligence."

"If we find out he's flesh and blood, I'm going to pay him off," Jo said.

"Joanna Pepperdine, that's a terrible idea. I already told you, if you give in without a fight, he's gonna keep coming back again and again. You'll never get rid of him. What if he keeps hammering away, he manages to find some sort of loophole and takes the farm?"

The blood drained from Jo's face. Delta had put her worst nightmare into words. She would gladly give the man money to go away, but the thought of him laying claim to her beloved farm was something that took her breath away, something she couldn't let happen.

"I...I need to take this one day at a time." Jo turned her computer on and clicked on a search site. She started with one of the more popular social profile sites and typed "Miles Parker" in the search section.

Several results popped up. Jo added California, which narrowed it down to a more manageable list. The first few weren't even close, and Jo was getting ready to give up when they hit pay dirt.

"That's him," Delta said. "I can't read anything. Let me go grab my reading glasses." She sprang from the chair and returned moments later, taking her spot next to Jo. "What does it say?"

Jo clicked on the profile. Another screen appeared, but there was limited information. "It's blocked. He has a private profile."

"Bummer." Delta stared at the screen. "Try the one with all of the pictures. Instant something."

"Instagram. I guess we could give it a try." Jo tapped the keys and pulled up another screen. "This one is showing even more results than the other one."

Jo attempted to sort through the names, but all of them were marked *private account*. "I would run a background check on him, but I don't recall Parker mentioning the area of California where he lived. I guess I'll wait to see what Chris finds."

"Try searching for the private investigator. What was his name?"

"I still have his card." Jo rummaged around in her top desk drawer and pulled out the business card. *Neil Garland, All Points Investigative Services, Wichita, Kansas.* She pressed the enter key, and a profile popped up. She double-clicked on the link and opened the file.

Garland's name and company name appeared at the top of the screen, along with a profile picture of the man Jo had met. "I think I found him."

"Bingo." Delta scooched her chair closer and leaned in for a closer look. "That's him all right."

Chapter 12

Jo read the words on the computer screen. "All Points Investigative Services. We specialize in adoption and finding missing persons. Reuniting loved ones for over thirty years."

"The company gets a high rating from the *Better Business Bureau*," Delta said.

"Yeah." Jo clicked through a few of the links, but nothing stood out, other than the fact that the company specialized in finding people. "We're back to square one." She shut the computer off and the women returned to the kitchen.

"If you don't need anything else, I was thinking about running a plate of chicken over to Gary's place," Delta said. "He sounded like he was coming down with a cold when he stopped by earlier, and I want to check on him."

"That's thoughtful of you." Jo's eyes twinkled mischievously. "So should I wait up for you to come home?"

"Don't look at me like that," Delta grunted. "I'm just being a good friend. I would do the same for any of you."

"And I think it's a wonderful gesture."

Delta pulled a to-go container from the fridge. She slipped her shoes on before grabbing the truck keys.

"Tell Gary I hope he's not coming down with something, but if he is, he doesn't need to come by to tend to the gardens tomorrow."

"Will do."

Jo followed Delta as far as the front porch where she found Duke in his favorite spot in front of the swing.

"Are you waiting for me?" Jo patted his head before settling onto the swing. Her eyes drifted to the mercantile. She thought about poor Sherry, how heartbroken the woman must be and the rejection she felt.

Her next thought was of Janet Ferris. Why would the woman confide to her boyfriend she felt threatened by Sherry? Perhaps Owen, Sherry's boyfriend, had made it up to throw suspicion on someone other than himself.

Was it possible there was more behind the altercation between Sherry and Janet, and Sherry was afraid to admit it because she already had a cloud of suspicion hanging over her?

There was also the mystery of why Janet went on a tangent at the gas station. According to what Marlee had told her, Janet claimed she was keeping her job at the gas station, she needed money, yet the employee Jo spoke to mentioned Janet had put in her notice.

Was it possible Janet had already lined up another job and just hadn't told Marlee? If so, why the big secret? Something wasn't adding up.

The fact Janet was strangled inside her car behind the deli was disturbing. Perhaps the killer had hidden in the back seat and then waited until Janet returned to the deli to take her out.

The deli's small rear parking lot was semi-secluded, and unless an employee was out there, very few people would be in the vicinity. Or...could it have been one of Janet's co-workers or even a customer who took her out?

What if someone witnessed the argument between Janet and Sherry and saw an opportunity to get rid of the woman? There were so many puzzle pieces still missing. Perhaps by the time Jo dropped Sherry off at work the following morning, she would have a better idea of what had happened to the woman.

The lights in Nash's workshop flickered and then went off. Moments later, Nash stepped outside. He glanced toward the house and then did a double take.

He gave Jo a wave and instead of heading to his apartment, he crossed the driveway and made his way to the porch.

"Hey, Nash."

"Hi, Jo. Do you mind if I join you?"

"Of course not." Jo slid over. "Duke and I decided to take advantage of the beautiful evening weather."

Nash patted Duke's head before joining Jo on the swing. "I saw Delta take off in the truck."

"She's delivering some leftovers to Gary. He mentioned feeling a little under the weather, and she wanted to check on him."

"Sounds like something Delta would do."

"She has a soft spot for him."

"You noticed, too?" Nash smiled. "I wasn't gonna say anything, but Gary stopped by the workshop a couple of days ago and asked me for some advice."

"About Delta?"

"He wondered what I thought about him asking Delta on a date."

"What did you tell him?"

"I told him he should go for it, and the worst that could happen is she said 'no.'"

Jo folded her hands; a slow smile crept across her face. "I think it's wonderful. It's never too late to find love."

"You don't say."

Jo shot Nash a quick glance. "You sound surprised."

"Surprised you would make that comment...an attractive woman like you, with no husband or family. I hope I'm not being too nosy, but you've never been married?"

Jo's heart skipped a beat. Nash wasn't just making conversation. He was genuinely curious.

"I was married once, a long time ago. It didn't work out. Gabe and I never had children. My

163

parents are dead, no siblings. I think that about covers my past history."

"I didn't mean to pry." Nash grew quiet as he stared at the field across the road.

"I'm sorry. I didn't mean to sound defensive. It's just...it was a long time ago." Since Nash had brought it up, Jo decided it was safe to ask a few questions of her own. "I know you have a son and an ex-wife. I'm surprised *you're* not married."

"I'm not ruling out marrying again. I just haven't found the right person...yet." Nash drummed his fingers on the armrest.

Jo could feel a warmth creep into her face and decided it was time to steer the conversation to safer ground. "Have you heard anything else about the death of the deli employee, Janet Ferris?"

"Yeah," Nash nodded. "I was at the hardware store earlier. Wayne Malton, the owner, and I were talking about it. The woman had some emotional issues."

"I heard the same. Sherry and Janet got into an argument hours before she was found dead in her car, out behind the deli. Deputy Franklin was by earlier to question Sherry. Janet's boyfriend told the authorities she claimed she was afraid of Sherry."

"Well, I hope they take a closer look at Owen, the boyfriend."

"I'm sure they are. I mean, she was living with him."

"The whole family should be investigated," Nash said.

"Why?"

"There was a big drug bust at the family compound early this spring. The cops hauled Owen's stepfather, Marty Zylstra, and Owen's uncle; I can't remember his name, off to jail. As far as I know, the uncle went to prison. The stepdad got off on a technicality."

Jo's scalp began to tingle. "Drugs?"

"Yeah. Street drugs and opioids. I don't know all of the details, but if Janet was as unstable as she appeared to be, it could be she was on drugs," Nash said.

"Wouldn't Marlee have tested her before hiring her?"

"In this small town?" Nash shrugged. "You could ask her."

"I wonder if she knew about the drug bust."

"She would have to."

The conversation drifted to the upcoming fall festival and Jo's plans to decorate. They discussed several projects around the farm, and the time flew by until Delta and the pickup truck coasted into the drive.

"Delta's back." Nash stood. "That's my signal to go. Thank you for allowing me to join you."

Jo's heart did a little flip-flop when their eyes met. "Thank you for asking. I thoroughly enjoyed our talk."

"Me, too. See you in the morning." Nash sauntered down the steps and strolled across the driveway, passing Delta on his way.

Jo waited until she was close. "Well? Was Gary surprised by his dinner delivery?"

"Yes. I didn't want him to eat alone, so I stayed to visit." Delta took the seat Nash had just vacated.

"How is he feeling?"

"Feeling?" Delta asked.

"You said he was feeling under the weather," Jo reminded her. "That's why you took him some food."

"Right. Right. Yeah. He's feeling better. He'll be here in the morning." Delta nodded toward Nash's workshop. "I see Nash and you were chatting. I didn't mean to scare him off."

"You didn't. He saw Duke and me over here and joined us. It's a nice night."

"What did you talk about?"

"This and that," Jo said vaguely. "We talked about the farm, some upcoming projects and the fall festival, among other things."

"Mmm. Hmm."

"Stop with the 'Mmm. Hmm.'"

"Fine." Delta picked at a piece of lint on her slacks. "I made my final decision. I'm going with the raspberry dream bars for the contest."

"You'll definitely give Marlee a run for her money," Jo predicted. "It's a divine recipe."

The sun disappeared behind the barn, and a cool breeze made Jo shiver. "I think it's time to go in."

"Yep."

Back inside, Jo grabbed a glass of water, and then Duke and she headed upstairs to bed while Delta headed to her room.

She brushed her teeth, thinking about her parents and their tumultuous relationship. Perhaps deep down they were the reason Jo was gun shy and anxious to avoid a commitment.

As she drifted off to sleep, she remembered Nash's words when he commented that he hadn't found the right person - yet.

Chapter 13

Jo's eyes flew open. She sat upright in bed, her heart pounding. It was the dream again - the dream where her mother was finally being released from prison and Jo was there, waiting to pick her up to take her home.

She could feel the excitement...her mother was finally free! She watched as her mother stepped through the open gate and began walking toward Jo, a smile on her face.

"Mom." Jo began walking quickly toward her mother. Before she could reach her, her mother collapsed on the ground.

"Mom!" Jo raced to her mother's side and fell to her knees. "Mom." She gently shook her; desperate for her mother to open her eyes, but it was no use. Her mother was gone.

Jo flipped on her bedside lamp. Her hand trembled as she reached for her glass of water. It had been months since she'd had the dream...her mother so close to freedom - just steps away and then she was gone.

She took a sip of water before turning the light off.

The sadness from the bad dream lingered. Jo couldn't shut her mind off as she thought about Miles Parker. What if Parker's claim of being Jo's half-brother was true? Would he have a leg to stand on and a legal right to her beloved farm? Delta was dead set against Jo paying him off to go away.

What had happened to Janet Ferris? Was someone who worked at the deli a killer? Why had the woman claimed she felt threatened by Sherry?

It was the wee hours of the morning before Jo finally drifted off to sleep, and it seemed as if she'd just fallen asleep when Duke began whining at the bedroom door.

"Hang on, Duke. I'm up." She stumbled out of bed and followed him to the front porch for a quick potty break. The sun peeked over the horizon, and beams of bright light filtered across the endless field of sunflowers in the field next door.

Jo paused to admire their beauty. "What beautiful sunflowers - God's magnificent creation," she told Duke.

She coaxed her pup back inside and to the kitchen where she filled his food and water dish, and then started a pot of coffee.

"You're up bright and early." Delta ambled into the kitchen. She let out a yawn and quickly covered her mouth. "Excuse me. I don't know what's going on, but I didn't sleep worth a hoot last night."

"Me, either," Jo confessed. "I spent half the night worrying about Miles Parker and the other half worrying about Sherry."

"And worrying about both of those didn't help one little bit, did it?" Delta poured a cup of coffee and pulled out a chair.

While the women enjoyed the quiet of the early morning, they discussed the fall festival and then the conversation drifted to Marlee and her employee's suspicious death. "While I was wide awake last night, I couldn't help but think about the authorities claim Janet was afraid of Sherry. It doesn't make any sense."

Delta lifted her cup and eyed her friend over the rim. "Jo, you and I both know the women here are always gonna have a target on their back. No two ways about it. Although, your plan to have the women start working outside the farm has been a success. Marlee appreciates Sherry and Sherry seems to enjoy the independence."

"Not to mention the extra money. Hopefully, this woman's death doesn't come back to bite Marlee or us." Jo finished the rest of her coffee and rinsed her cup before heading upstairs to get ready for the day.

After finishing, she grabbed her cell phone and noticed she'd missed a call. It was from Marlee, asking her to return the call.

She dialed her friend's number. "Hey, Marlee."

"Hello, Jo. Thanks for calling me back."

"Is everything all right?"

"Yes. I mean, I hope so. When I got to work this morning, I found the back door ajar. Someone was inside the deli last night after we closed."

"They broke in?"

"More like sneaked in. There's no sign of forced entry...the door was ajar."

"That's odd." Jo remembered how Marlee mentioned feeling forgetful. "Do you think it's possible you forgot to lock up?"

"Maybe. I've been forgetting a lot lately." There was a hint of relief in Marlee's voice. "Yes, I'm sure that was it. I called to say I want Sherry to take today off. She's been working a lot of extra hours, and I think she could use a break. She can come in tomorrow to cover her scheduled shift. "

"Are you sure?"

"Yes. I have today's shifts covered."

The women chatted for a few more minutes before Marlee told her she needed to get to work.

Jo told her good-bye and then headed downstairs where Delta was on the move, zipping back and forth from the counter to the stove. Jo pitched in to help, and they finished breakfast just in time for the women to arrive.

Sherry was the last to show up, looking glum.

Jo pulled her aside. "Is everything all right?"

"I can't stop thinking about Janet's death. I think I jinxed Marlee."

"You did not jinx Marlee. You have to put that thought out of your head," Jo said. "I talked to Marlee this morning. She wants you to take the day off and I agree."

"She doesn't want me anymore?" A look of panic crossed Sherry's face.

"No. We both agreed you need a day off. You're still scheduled to work tomorrow. If truth be told, Marlee could probably use a break, too."

During breakfast, Jo was quiet as she mulled over the latest event. Had someone managed to sneak into the deli the previous night? If so, why?

"Earth to Jo." Delta, who was sitting on Jo's right, snapped her fingers in front of her face.

"Sorry. I'm a little preoccupied." Jo forced herself to pay attention to the conversations, pushing Marlee's latest incident from her mind.

After breakfast, Sherry and the other women offered to clean up the kitchen while Jo motioned for Delta to follow her to the front porch. She waited until they were off to the side and out of earshot. "I didn't want to say anything in front of the women. I talked to Marlee this morning. She said when she got to the deli, the back door was ajar."

"Oh no. Someone broke in?" Delta asked.

"Marlee wasn't sure if she'd forgotten to lock up last night or if someone sneaked in," Jo said. "What if Marlee or her employees are potential targets?"

"Meaning you think someone may be trying to scare Marlee or Sherry? I hate to say it, but it seems like these incidents are ramping up ever since Marlee hired Sherry," Delta said. "Maybe she's not gonna be safe there."

"I hadn't thought of it like that." Jo tapped her foot on the floor. Had she unintentionally put a target on Sherry or Marlee's back? Was it possible someone in Divine was dead set on getting rid of Sherry by throwing suspicion on her as a potential killer? "I need to talk to Marlee."

"What time is Sherry scheduled to start work?" Delta asked.

"She's not working today. Marlee suggested - and I agreed - that Sherry needed a day off, to give her a break from all of the stress."

"It's eight-thirty now," Delta said. "Why don't you make a quick trip to town, to talk to Marlee in private?"

"Yes, I think I will."

Delta returned to the kitchen while Jo ran upstairs to take a quick shower and throw on a pair of shorts and button down blouse. By the time she returned to the kitchen, it was empty except for Delta and her helper for the day, Michelle.

"I'll be back in a little while." Jo grabbed her keys on the way out. During the drive to town, she prayed for Marlee, she prayed for Sherry, who now not only had a co-worker's suspicious death hanging over her head, but her family had also outright rejected her after she sought their forgiveness.

It was a tough spot, and Jo felt responsible for both issues...for encouraging Sherry to make the first move and contact her family and for her taking the job at the deli.

Perhaps it wasn't such a brilliant idea, after all, to have the women seek employment beyond the safe confines of Jo's watchful eye. But then again someday soon, all of them would be forced to handle tough situations, and Jo wouldn't be around.

At least this way, she could still be involved in the process, but so far, it wasn't the resounding success Jo had hoped it would be.

When she reached the deli, Jo exited the vehicle and circled around to the back of the building. The rear door was ajar, and she could hear clanging coming from the kitchen. "Hello? Marlee?"

Jo hesitantly reached for the handle when the screen door flew open, and a harried Marlee appeared in the doorway. "Hey, Jo."

"Hi, Marlee. I'm sorry to bother you."

"You're not bothering me." Marlee motioned for Jo to follow her into the kitchen. "C'mon in. I have something I want to show you."

Jo waved to Carlos, the cook, as she followed Marlee through the kitchen and then the server's station before entering a small hall. They passed by the restrooms and another door until they reached the end of the hall.

"Over here." Marlee crossed the room and paused when she reached a wall of lockers. "Check it out. It looks like someone tried to pry this locker open. Remember me mentioning earlier that the back door was ajar when I got here? I think someone was trying to get into the lockers."

"That's odd."

"I have a master key." Marlee reached inside her pocket and pulled out a keyring.

"Have you...looked to see what's inside them?"

"Not yet." Marlee unlocked the first locker. A work apron and a pair of black sneakers were inside. She closed the locker and unlocked the one next to it. "Empty. This was Janet's locker."

Marlee started to close the door, and then pulled it back open. "Wait. There's something way back in the corner." She reached her hand inside. "It's stuck." She shifted her weight "I...got it."

She pulled out a small notebook.

Jo peered over her shoulder as she flipped it open. Inside were initials, followed by a series of cryptic numbers and dates. "KA, BV, SM, OC and Ace."

"What does this mean?" Marlee whispered. "You don't think whoever was back here was looking for this, do you?"

"I have no idea. Ace sounds like a nickname," Jo said.

"I've never heard it before."

"The authorities will want this notebook for their investigation. Maybe you should take a quick snapshot of the notes, just in case."

"Good idea, except my cell phone is dead."

"You can use mine." Jo handed Marlee her cell phone. "I'll send you copies."

Marlee snapped several pictures of the pages and then slid the notebook back inside the locker before shutting it.

The last locker contained a book of poetry and a packet of Kleenex. "This must be Sherry's locker," Marlee said. "I've seen her with the poetry."

"Sherry feels terrible." Jo watched Marlee shut the locker. "She's convinced she somehow jinxed you and the deli."

"That's crazy. Sherry hasn't jinxed this place, but I'm beginning to suspect Janet's death and the possible break-in are somehow related."

"I agree." Jo stepped into the hall. "Do you still want Sherry to work tomorrow?"

"Yes. If she can be here in the morning, right after the breakfast rush, that would be wonderful."

The women stopped by Marlee's small office to call Detective Beck, the man in charge of Janet's investigation. Marlee left a brief message, telling him she found a notebook wedged in the back of Janet's locker.

Jo glanced at her watch. "I better let you get back to work."

When she reached the farm, she made a beeline for Sherry's apartment. She wasn't there, so Jo stopped by the bakeshop and mercantile. The women working hadn't seen her since breakfast.

"Check with Nash," Leah suggested. "I think she was trying to find somewhere to fill in since she wasn't needed at the deli."

Jo thanked Leah for the tip and made her way to Nash's workshop. Nash and Sherry were inside.

"Hey, Jo." Nash's face lit. "What's up?"

"Nothing much. I was hoping to speak to Sherry for a moment."

"Of course."

Sherry removed her work gloves and followed Jo outside. "Is everything okay?"

"Yes. I wanted to let you know Marlee asked if you could come in tomorrow morning at ten-thirty."

"Of course." Sherry's expression brightened. "I...yes."

"There's something else." Jo explained how someone had attempted to gain access to the employee lockers.

"Can you think of anything one of the other employees may have had inside their lockers that would cause someone to want to break in?"

Sherry started to shake her head and then stopped, her eyes growing wide. "Well, now that you mention it, Janet may have had something inside hers."

Chapter 14

"What was inside Janet's locker?" Jo asked.

"Lottery tickets...the scratch-off kind. Every time I saw her on break, she was scratching tickets, and it was kind of odd because she kept this little notebook with her, too." Sherry shrugged. "Maybe she kept a record of her winnings."

"Was the notebook blue and white?"

"Yeah. How did you know?" Sherry asked.

"Marlee and I found a notebook wedged in the back of Janet's locker. It was full of initials, dates and numbers."

"Maybe she was in some sort of lottery pool. The book was a way to track the players and the winnings."

"It's possible." Jo nodded absentmindedly. She thanked Sherry for the information and reminded her that Marlee would need her the following morning.

After she left, Jo wandered around the yard, inspecting her flowering plants. The first frost was right around the corner, and soon the blooms would start to die. This would be Jo's first winter in Divine, although she was familiar with the weather in Wichita.

"Whatcha doing?" Delta joined her near the flowerbeds with a tray of treats in hand.

"Just checking out the flowerbeds." Jo straightened her back.

"How is Marlee?"

"Stressed out. Remember how I mentioned she found the deli's back door ajar?"

"Yeah."

"Someone attempted to access the employees' lockers. We found a notebook wedged in the back of Janet's locker. I spoke with Sherry, and she said it belonged to Janet."

Jo also told her how the woman spent her breaks scratching lottery tickets. "Inside the notebook were initials, dates, numbers and the name Ace."

"Huh." Delta shifted the tray to her other hand.

"Does the name Ace ring a bell?"

Delta shook her head. "Nope. Sounds like a nickname."

Jo pulled a weed growing next to a hosta plant. "I took pictures of the notes in the notebook. Maybe we could look at it together. Now that I think about it, I need to text a copy to Marlee." She tossed the small pile of weeds in the field next to the house and joined Delta on the porch. "Something tells me there's some sort of clue in the notebook."

She sent the pictures to her friend, and her cell phone rang seconds later. An out of breath Marlee was on the other end. "I was getting ready to call you."

"You found something out. The police figured out who murdered Janet."

"No, but she was under investigation for stealing from the gas station. You'll never guess what she was stealing."

"Scratch-off lottery tickets."

Marlee was silent for a moment. "How...did you know?"

"Because I just spoke with Sherry. She told me Janet was big into scratch-off tickets. Every time she was on break, the woman was scratching tickets."

"Stealing them and then scratching them," Marlee said. "What if she freaked out and went crazy in the gas station after finding out the management was investigating lottery ticket thefts?"

"It's certainly possible. I was thinking the notebook may have been some sort of cryptic coding system for Janet to keep track of the tickets," Jo said. "I sent you copies."

"Thanks. I'll take a look at them later."

"Delta and I are going to take a look at the notes, too." Jo turned to Delta after telling her friend good-bye. "Investigators suspect Janet was stealing lottery tickets from the gas station."

"That's crazy. Wouldn't she know she would eventually get busted?"

"Maybe she hoped by the time the authorities could pin the thefts on her, she would be long gone," Jo forwarded the photos from her cell phone to her email and then headed to her office to print them off.

She joined Delta on the porch and handed her one of the sheets.

Delta slipped her reading glasses on. "I can't make heads or tails of this. It's written in some sort of code...there are initials, dates, numbers. Ace...who is Ace?"

"I have no idea. Maybe it's a nickname for someone, Janet's partner in the thefts. Marlee didn't recognize the name."

"What if Janet was in on the scratch-off scheme with a gas station co-worker? We need to figure out who or what Ace is."

"I have an idea." Delta consulted her watch. "Since Marlee has never heard the name, there's a chance it has something to do with the gas station."

"Let me guess...we suddenly need gas," Jo said. "We filled up the last time we were there snooping around."

"Then let's take the truck. I think it's due for a fill-up." Delta didn't wait for Jo to reply and headed toward the door.

Jo stopped by the workshop to let Nash know they were leaving. He gave her an odd look. "Weren't you just out?"

"Yes, but Delta wants to run into town, and I thought I would keep her company." Jo hurried out of the workshop before Nash could ask more questions.

Delta was already waiting by the truck. "You drive." Jo made her way to the passenger side while her friend climbed behind the wheel.

"I think this Ace may be our link," Delta said. "Maybe Ace was Janet's scratch-off partner and thought she had a stash of unscratched tickets in her locker."

"It's possible."

On their way to the gas station, Delta swung by the post office to mail some packages. They passed by *Divine Delicatessen* and then pulled into *Four Corners Mini-Mart* and parked next to a pump.

"I'll pump the gas while you run in and ask about Ace," Jo said.

"Sounds like a plan." Delta gave Jo a mock salute and strode to the front door of the store.

She returned before Jo had finished filling the tank, her face red as she darted across the parking lot. "We were on the money."

"Ace works here." Jo replaced the nozzle and gas cap before grabbing her receipt.

"She's the assistant manager."

"Ace is a woman?"

"Ace is the nickname for Ashley Edison. She called in sick and isn't working today," Delta said.

"Interesting. Do you think she knows about the lottery ticket investigation and skipped town?"

"I don't know, but I think it's definitely worth doing a little digging around."

"I'm sure the authorities are one step ahead of us." Jo climbed into the pickup and pulled the door shut. She waited for Delta to join her. "What if Janet and Ace teamed up to steal the tickets? There was some sort of argument. Ace knew about the notebook, so she broke into the deli to try to get it back."

The women returned home, just in time for Delta to start working on dinner.

"I haven't heard back from Chris. I figured he would have called me by now. Maybe he sent an email instead." Jo headed to her office to check, but there was nothing from the attorney.

She wandered back to the kitchen where Leah was helping Delta, so she made her way upstairs to the attic, one of her current projects.

Despite her initial excitement over the book nook, Miles Parker's claim loomed over Jo's head like a big, black cloud. It was terrifying to think that this man...a complete stranger...might have a legitimate claim to her farm.

She mentally shook her head, but the feeling of impending doom refused to go away. Jo returned downstairs to her office. She glanced at the cell phone on the desk and noticed she'd missed a call. The call was from Chris.

Jo entered her password to unlock her phone, her heart pounding. She prayed a quick prayer for good news.

She pressed the button and listened to the message. "Hey, Jo. Chris here. I have some information to share with you. Please call me back at your earliest convenience." Jo could tell from the tone of Chris's voice that something was wrong.

Jo sucked in a breath and started to dial his number. She disconnected before she finished dialing and headed to the kitchen.

Delta gave Jo a quick look before giving her friend her full attention. "What's wrong?"

"I...the attorney called me back. I mean, he left a message, and he wants me to call him."

Delta hastily wiped her hands on her apron. "You need a little moral support?"

"Yes." Jo nodded, her breath catching in her throat. "If you don't mind."

"I'll be right back, Leah." Delta put a light hand on Jo's back and gently led her to the office.

Delta closed the door behind them and then pulled her chair around to the other side of the desk. "Now, we're gonna sit here for a minute and catch our breath. We're not gonna panic, no matter what the lawyer says."

"Right." Jo pressed her hands to her cheeks. "I'm going to remain calm." Even though she said the words, she could feel panic rising in her like a tidal wave. "I feel like I'm standing on the edge of a cliff - like something is about to happen, and it's going to change my life forever."

"Let's pray." Delta's warm hand clasped Jo's, and the women bowed their heads. "Dear Heavenly Father. We pray for Jo now, Lord. You know her situation, her fear someone, a total stranger is trying to make their way into her life, to lay claim to not only Jo's inheritance but also everything that she holds dear. Lord, we pray whatever news we're about to get, that you'll turn it into a blessing, for Jo, for *Second Chance,* for the farm and all who live here."

"Amen."

"Amen." Jo lifted her head and sucked in a shaky breath as she reached for the phone. "Let's get this over with."

Chapter 15

"Thank you for calling Nyles and Hartman. How can I help you?"

"Yes. This is Jo...Joanna Pepperdine. I'm returning a call from Chris Nyles."

"Hold for a moment. I'll see if he's available to take your call."

Jo squeezed her eyes shut as Delta patted her arm. "It's gonna be okay. No matter what."

"I hope so."

"Hey, Jo." Chris's voice boomed on the other end. "Thanks for calling me back."

"I listened to your message. Do you mind if I put you on speaker? I'm here with my friend, Delta, and would like her to hear what you have to say, as well."

"Yes, of course." Chris cleared his throat. "I was thinking it might be best if I stop by your place."

Jo could hear rustling on the other end of the line. "I have a few free hours this afternoon, and I've been meaning to check out your farm. Would it be possible for me to swing by around three this afternoon?"

Jo consulted the clock. It would take Chris close to two hours just to get there. "Yes. That will be fine. Would you like to stay for dinner?"

"Thanks, but I have a dinner meeting in Topeka this evening. I'll only be able to stay for a tour and a brief meeting."

"I understand. Yes. I'll be here. Thank you, Chris."

"You're welcome, Jo. I'll see you in a couple of hours."

Jo thanked him again and disconnected the call. She waved her cell phone at Delta. "Chris would not drive almost two hours from his office if he had good news." She jumped out of the chair and strode to the window. "What am I going to do?"

"I can tell you what you're *not* going to do." Delta joined her. "You're not going to panic. We wait until your lawyer fills us in on what's going on."

Duke trotted into the room. He greeted Delta and then nudged Jo's hand.

"Duke could use a little fresh air, and I think you could, too. Why don't you two take a walk and clear your head?" Delta suggested.

"You're right. Fresh air sounds good." Duke and Jo wandered out the back door. They passed by the mercantile and began walking past Nash's workshop.

The door was open, and the sound of a table saw echoed from inside. Jo approached the open door and could see Nash, along with Kelli, standing in front of the workbench.

Nash must have sensed Jo's presence, and he turned. "Hey, Jo."

Jo grinned at his safety goggles, pushing his cropped locks up and his hair standing on end. "Hi, Nash. I didn't mean to bother you. Duke and I were getting ready to take a walk out back and heard some noise, so we figured we would stop by to see what you're up to."

"Not much. We were trimming some boards." Nash removed the goggles. "We were getting ready to take a break."

Kelli removed her goggles and touched Nash's arm. "I don't need to take a break. I'm just as happy to hang out here with you."

"I appreciate that," Nash gave her a warm smile. "I wouldn't mind stretching my legs."

"You're welcome to walk out back with Duke and me," Jo offered.

"I think I will." Nash motioned to Kelli. "We'll finish our project when I get back."

Kelli made a small noise and frowned. Jo started to invite her to join them, but Nash had already crossed the room and stepped out of the building. "We shouldn't be more than half an hour."

They left Kelli standing in the doorway and circled the side of the workshop, passing by Gary's gardening shed as Duke led the way.

"We could've invited Kelli along," Jo said.

"I suppose, but you know the saying...three's a crowd," Nash teased.

Jo was certain Nash was flirting with her, and her cheeks turned a shade of pink. "I guess we can't count Duke, then."

"Nope. Duke doesn't count."

The couple reached the two-lane path leading to the back of the property and fell into step.

"Have you found anything else out about the woman who died the other day?"

"Janet Ferris," Jo said. "Sherry is a suspect in her death. I questioned Sherry, and she told me that the woman was always scratching lottery tickets on her breaks. Come to find out, the store owner was investigating missing lottery scratch-offs."

"So Janet was stealing the tickets," Nash said.

"It's possible," Jo agreed.

"But it would be hard to prove, now that she's dead. Not to mention someone else would've had knowledge of the thefts. The station must keep an inventory of the tickets."

"This is where it starts to get interesting. Delta and I stopped by to get gas earlier. The assistant manager, Ashley Edison, didn't show up for work today."

"So she may have been involved in the thefts," Nash theorized.

Jo told him Marlee searched the deli employees' lockers and discovered a notebook with notes inside Janet's locker. "There were dates, initials and numbers. We couldn't make heads or tails of it, except for the name 'Ace.'"

"Ace?"

"Ashley Edison. That's her nickname," Jo said. "What if Ashley, the assistant manager at the gas station, and Janet, an employee, were stealing scratch-off tickets? Something happened, Ashley murdered Janet and now Ashley is on the run."

"Whew." Nash blew air through thinned lips. "If that's the case, I don't think those women thought it through, that they would eventually get caught."

"Unless they planned on hitting the 'big one,' paying the money for the stolen..."

"Borrowed," Nash quipped.

"Borrowed lottery tickets so no one would be the wiser."

The couple reached the first garden and Jo began inspecting the tidy rows of vegetables.

Nash stood watching from the side. "Won't be long and the gardens will be done until spring."

"Yes." Jo brushed off her hands. "I'll have to figure out a way to keep Gary busy during the winter months, so he doesn't get lonely and bored."

"I think Delta will take care of that." Nash waited for Jo to step out of the garden.

They stopped briefly to inspect the bee boxes, and Jo admired the new platforms. Nash had recently rebuilt them after a near catastrophe when one of them tipped over and a bunch of angry bees swarmed the box.

Their next stop was the larger of the two gardens.

Jo paused to admire the sunflowers. "These are my favorite, and after all, this is the Sunflower State." She rubbed a light hand along the petals. "I wonder what we could use them for."

"Sunflower oil. I've even heard of sunflower seed coffee. If you plan to harvest the seeds, you'll need to protect them. The birds and butterflies are attracted to the nectar." Nash explained once the seeds were almost ready to harvest, he heard covering them with a plastic bag to keep the birds from eating them was necessary. "I guess you better talk to Gary. He's the green thumb around here."

Duke patrolled the perimeter of the garden before trotting to the fence.

"Stay on this side, Duke." Out of the corner of her eye, Jo caught a sudden movement farther down the fence line. From a distance, it looked like a man...tall and with broad shoulders. She lifted her gaze in an attempt to catch a glimpse of his face when the sun suddenly blinded her.

She blinked a couple of times. When she looked again, the man was gone. "Did you see that?"

"See what?" Nash who had been kneeling next to a tomato plant, stood.

"That man. There was a man standing over there." Jo pointed to the fence. "He was tall...really tall. I tried to see his face, but the sun was blinding me. When I looked again, he was gone."

"Are you sure?" Nash jogged to the fence line, and Jo hurried after him.

"He was right here." Jo craned her neck and peered down the fence line. "There's no one here."

Nash motioned to the open field. "He couldn't have disappeared that fast. Are you sure your eyes aren't playing tricks on you?"

Jo frowned. "No. I could've sworn..." Her voice trailed off. "I guess I was seeing things." She glanced at her watch. "We should head back before Kelli sends out a search party. I have an appointment at three o'clock."

She cast a final glance over her shoulder in the direction of where she had seen the stranger. The hair on her arms shot up, and she got the distinct feeling someone was still there. Jo mentally shrugged it off. Maybe her eyes...and her mind were playing tricks on her.

Nash and Jo wandered toward the front of the farm. They stopped when they reached the bakeshop.

"Thank you for going with me."

Nash smiled, the dimple in his chin deepening. "I enjoyed the walk and the chat. Anytime you ever want a little company, come look me up."

Jo's heart did a mini summersault as their eyes met. "Yes...I'll be sure to do that."

She waited for Nash to return to the workshop, and then slowly made her way to the kitchen, which was empty.

Jo continued through the dining room to the living room. She found Delta sitting in the recliner. There were two big boxes on the floor in front of her.

"Whatcha doing?" Jo eased onto the sofa and tucked her feet underneath her.

"Sorting through these books someone donated to the mercantile. I figured you might want to go through them first to see if you want any of them for your book nook."

Jo reached into one of the boxes and pulled out a hardcover book. "Thanks, Delta. I love old books." She held the book close and breathed deeply. "I love the smell. I love the feel of a book in my hands." She glanced at the cover and set the book back inside the box. "Have you found anything interesting?"

"As a matter of fact...this one has your name written all over it." Delta reached behind her, pulled out a book and handed it to Jo.

"Love Unexpected. 12 Steps to Building a Forever Relationship with the Man of your Dreams." Jo snorted. "What's this?"

"For you and Nash. Once you two realize you have a match made in heaven, this book will give you pointers on how to keep the fires burning."

"Very funny." Jo handed the book back and cast an anxious glance at the front door. "Chris should be here anytime now." She wandered out onto the front porch and the swing.

Chris would not have made a special trip and driven all the way to Divine just to give Jo good news. There was something to Miles Parker's claim. A feeling of dread settled in the pit of her stomach.

Could this man - a complete stranger - lay claim to her home...to her inheritance? What would become of the farm? Of the women? The more she thought of the "what ifs," the more her stomach churned until she felt like throwing up.

The door banged shut, and Delta joined her. "No sign of your lawyer friend yet?"

"No. He'll be here."

Delta meandered across the porch and plunked down on the other end of the swing. "You look pasty white."

"I feel like throwing up."

"Can't say as I blame you." Delta tugged on her apron. "I've been thinking about this mess."

"Yeah?"

"Well, the man can't take everything you have, even if you do have the same father."

"It's not *if* he can take something from me. It's *what* he might take from me." Jo swallowed hard, remembering the look on Parker's face as he gazed around the farm. She remembered the comment he made about Jo's businesses and how he would enjoy living in Divine.

"He's trying to scare you. Maybe you're right. Money talks. That fancy lawyer of yours can probably draw up some crafty paperwork. You give Mr. Parker some cash; he signs off on any future rights and..." Delta snapped her fingers, "you never hear from him again."

Before Jo could reply, a black four-door sedan pulled into the driveway. She stood. "Chris is here."

Chapter 16

Jo waited for Chris, the man who had stuck by her side following her father's death as well as her mother's trial and eventual incarceration, to step out of his car.

He had not only been a shoulder to lean on; he'd been instrumental in helping her get *Second Chance* up and running.

The process of handling the paperwork to open the halfway house and obtaining licenses to operate multiple businesses at the property had been daunting. Chris had been a huge help in navigating the legalities.

She hurried down the steps and darted to the driver's side of the car. The two embraced, and then Jo took a step back, grinning mischievously. "I almost didn't recognize you. I know it hasn't been that long, but it seems like forever since I saw you."

"It's the hair." Chris patted the sides of his graying locks. "Business at the law firm has been busier than usual, and it's aging me."

"Maybe you should retire."

"And miss out on all of the fun?"

Jo and Chris strolled toward the house and stepped onto the porch where Delta stood waiting.

"Chris, this is my close friend, Delta. She's also the chief cook and bottle washer around this joint."

"It's my pleasure." Chris grasped Delta's hand. "Are you keeping this troublemaker in line?"

"I sure do try." Delta pumped his hand. "My goodness, Jo. You never told me your attorney was such a looker."

Chris chuckled. "I'll take that as a compliment."

Delta continued gripping his hand. "Honey, you can take it any way you want. Are you single?"

"Delta," Jo gasped.

"What? There's no harm in asking." Delta finally released her grip. "We got some very nice ladies living here at the farm, all of whom are single."

"As a matter of fact, I'm a widower. My wife passed away a few years ago. I have two children and a couple of grandchildren. Would you like their names and ages?" he teased.

"We can delve into your background another time." Delta motioned toward the house. "You sure you can't stay for supper?"

"Delta is an excellent cook," Jo said.

"As much as I would like to, I have a dinner meeting in the city. Perhaps next time." Chris patted his flat stomach as he glanced around. "The place looks great. I wouldn't mind taking a tour."

"Of course. We'll take a tour first, and then we'll discuss what you found out."

Chris smiled. "You never were one to beat around the bush. Yes, as soon as you give me a tour, I'll fill you in."

"I'll make a pot of coffee." Delta stepped back inside the house.

Jo started the tour inside *Divine Baked Goods Shop* before showing him around *Second Chance Mercantile*. The next stop was Nash's workshop where Nash and Kelli were inside working.

There was a brief introduction before Jo led him to the women's units in the back.

"How many residents are you housing, Jo?"

"Six. That's all I have room for. I may expand sometime down the road." An unsettling feeling filled Jo as she remembered the reason Chris was there. "We'll head back to the house and go over what you found. I'm sure you want to be on your way. You still have a few hours of driving left today."

They returned to the house. After a quick tour of her Victorian home, Jo led him into the kitchen.

214

Delta had the coffee ready. The cups were sitting on the kitchen table along with an array of decadent treats. She poured them each a cup.

"Thank you." Chris eyed the plate of goodies. "Did you make these?"

"Sure did. I do all of the baking for the baked goods shop right here in the kitchen." Delta pointed to her raspberry dream bars. "If you like raspberry, you might want to try one of those."

Chris eased one of the bars off the plate and took a big bite. "This is delicious."

"Delta is thinking of entering her raspberry bars in Divine's fall festival baking contest," Jo said.

"I would pick these hands down as the winner." Chris took another big bite.

Delta beamed. "So you like them?"

"Like them? I love them."

"I'll stick a few in a to-go container, and you can take them with you." Delta hurried to the cupboard.

"You don't have to," Chris protested.

"I insist. Besides, you did Jo a big favor by driving all the way out here." Delta began transferring several of the bars from the plate to the container.

"Speaking of which..." Jo's expression grew solemn. "It's not good news, is it?"

Chris reached for his napkin and wiped the corners of his mouth. "I'm sorry, Jo. I did some preliminary research. I believe there's a chance Miles Parker is telling the truth."

"You believe my father is also his father?" Jo could feel the blood drain from her face.

"I contacted the private investigator, Neil Garland. In fact, my partner is familiar with Neil and his company. He's a straight shooter. I met him at his office. He was forthright in his assertion and knowledge of the information."

Delta set the container on the table. "You're going to take their word for it?"

"No. After he shared the information on his client, I did some digging around on my own. Your father employed Irene Parker during the dates in question. As Miles indicated, he and his mother moved to California not long after his birth."

"But we don't know one hundred percent that he's not lying," Jo insisted.

"No, we don't," Chris agreed. "Has Mr. Parker contacted you again?"

"No." Jo pressed a hand to her chest as the room began to spin. "He will though. I'm sure of it. He wants to take the farm." She began to ramble, spilling out all of her fears.

Chris listened quietly before reaching for both of her hands. "Joanna, I'm sure this news is shocking, but you're nowhere near handing a red cent over to this man."

"Maybe I should just pay him off to go away."

"I don't believe that is a wise decision. I know you're freaked out, and I don't blame you, but we have to be very careful. This may be a cunning ploy by Parker to get his hands on your money."

"What...what do you suggest that I do?"

"Nothing. We let Mr. Parker make the next move."

"Wait for him to contact me again."

"Yes. We wait to see what happens, and then we go from there," Chris said.

Jo's hand trembled as she reached for her coffee, her thoughts racing. The only thing she could think was Miles Parker, a complete stranger, had blindsided her and was going to take everything she loved away from her.

"I'll do whatever you suggest." Jo slowly pushed her chair back and stood. "How long do you think he'll wait before contacting me again?"

"It's hard telling." Chris shrugged. "Could be today, tomorrow, or it might be months."

"But you don't think he'll wait long."

"No, not if he has a legitimate claim. Your family's estate went through probate after your mother's death. Technically, he doesn't have a right to your money, but then again…"

"If he finds the right attorney, he might give it a go," Delta guessed.

"Yes." Chris followed suit and stood. "I'm sorry to be the bearer of bad news, Jo. I don't want you to panic."

"At least not yet," Jo said.

"Right. At least not yet." Chris glanced at his watch. "I've got to get going if I want to make it to my next meeting on time."

Delta handed Chris the container of treats. "You're welcome to come back here and join us for dinner."

"I would like that." Chris shot Delta one of his most engaging smiles, and Jo could've sworn her friend started to swoon.

Jo led Chris through the house and onto the front porch. "Thank you so much for making the long drive over here. I know this was out of your way. Please...you must send me a bill for your time, for the research and for everything you've done."

Chris placed a light hand on her arm. "You're my friend, and I'm thrilled to be able to help out a friend." He dropped his hand. "It's good to see you, Jo. I've missed our chats and have been meaning to call you."

"I've missed you, too. A lot has happened since the last time I saw you."

"For the better." Chris nodded in the direction of the mercantile and bakeshop. "You're doing a wonderful thing with these women. Your mother would be proud of you."

Jo smiled sadly. "I like to think she's up in heaven, cheering me on."

Chris gave her a warm hug. "I'm sure she is." He took a quick step back as Jo swiped at her eyes.

"Are you going to be all right?" A concerned look crossed his face.

"Yes." Jo nodded. "I'll be fine."

Chris patted his pocket. "You have my cell phone number."

"Yes."

"Call me as soon as you hear from Mr. Parker again...and don't agree to anything he asks or demands until we talk. Promise?"

"Yes, I promise."

"Thank Delta again for the goodies. We'll talk soon."

Jo's expression was thoughtful as she watched Chris climb into his vehicle. She waited until his car disappeared from sight before returning inside.

She hesitated when she reached the living room and could hear Delta banging around in the kitchen. Jo drifted into her office for a few quiet minutes to sort through her jumbled emotions. She eased onto her chair and stared out the window.

"There you are." Delta appeared in the doorway. "Are you gonna be okay?"

Jo swiveled to face her friend. "Do you think he could take everything from me?"

"No." Delta didn't wait for an invitation and sank down in the chair across from Jo. "Mr. Nyles is on your side. I can't imagine he'll let that happen."

"I hope not."

"I know you're upset, but you mustn't let fear take hold," Delta said. "We don't know what is going to happen."

"That's the scary part," Jo sighed. "The unknown. Chris would not have driven all the way out here if he wasn't concerned."

"Really?" Delta lifted a brow. "He came to see you."

"Seriously. Chris is a friend...just like Nash is a friend." Jo threw her hands up in exasperation. "Does everything have to have a romantic angle to it?"

Delta pointed to her eyes. "I see things a little differently than you, with my eyes wide open."

"Oh, brother. I have some work to do."

"And I've got me a pot of hearty beans to make." Delta headed back to the kitchen while Jo sorted through her emails and handled some paperwork, all the while in the back of her mind she wondered about Miles Parker, not "if" he would contact her but when.

Jo's gut told her it was only a matter of time before the other shoe dropped. She hoped she would be mentally prepared for it when it did.

The evening meal was the bright spot of Jo's day, as the women gathered around the table. Nash was notably absent. Kelli told her he had some errands to run and wouldn't be back in time for dinner.

Tara regaled the women with tales of her first day mishaps in the mercantile when she accidentally showed a customer to the broom closet instead of the restroom and then was mortified to discover she had erroneously given directions to downtown Divine instead of the area's focal point - the center of the contiguous forty-eight states.

After dinner, Jo helped clean up and then headed to her room, claiming she was feeling under the weather.

Delta gave her a knowing look, but didn't put up a fuss. Instead, she told her to let her know if she needed anything.

Jo changed into her pajamas. She curled up in bed and switched the television on.

There was a pawing at the door. Jo climbed back out to let Duke in. He gave her an unhappy face and let out a grunt, a clear indication of his disapproval at being left in the hall.

"Sorry, buddy. I didn't think you were ready for bed."

He jumped onto the bed while Jo returned to her spot. She began flipping through the channels when her cell phone, plugged into her charger next to her bed, began beeping.

She gave it a quick glance and attempted to ignore it. It beeped a second, and then a third time. "What is going on?"

Jo grabbed the cell phone, squinting her eyes as she studied the screen. It was a text message from Marlee. Her eyes grew wide when she clicked on the message and began reading the text.

"Oh no!"

Chapter 17

Ashley Edison is missing. Someone broke into her home.

It took a second for Ashley's name to register. Jo scrolled until she found Marlee's cell phone number and pressed the call button.

"You got my text?"

"Ashley Edison, the assistant manager of the mini-mart/gas station, is missing?"

"Yes. She lives with her mother. When her mother arrived home today, she found Ashley's car parked in the driveway and the front door busted."

"But there's no sign of the woman?"

"Nope. Whoever broke in tore the place apart."

"Wow." Jo rubbed the end of her nose. "I figured she was the one who was responsible or at least involved in Janet's death."

"It looks like she's been kidnapped."

"Have you had time to take a look at the pictures of Janet's notebook?"

"The investigators were here earlier to pick it up. I looked at the pictures you sent but I couldn't make heads or tails of them." Marlee continued. "I'm stopping by Owen Cole's place tomorrow morning to tell him how sorry I am about Janet's death, to offer my condolences and to bring him some food."

"You don't think he's holding you responsible for Janet's death, do you?" It was something Jo hadn't thought of until that moment.

"It has crossed my mind," Marlee admitted. "After all, she was found on my property, and the authorities are still investigating."

Jo didn't say it to Marlee, but the fact the woman was Marlee's employee and was found murdered on her property could set her up for a potential lawsuit. The possibilities were endless if the right attorney came along and thought the family might have a case.

"Would you like me to tag along when you visit him?" Jo asked.

"I...that's very nice of you to offer, Jo. Yes, it might not be a bad idea to have someone with me. I'm not sure what kind of reception I'm going to get."

"What time were you thinking?"

"Well, if you drop Sherry off in the morning to start the shift right after the breakfast rush, we can leave when you get here around ten-thirty. I don't want him to think I don't care."

"I'm sure he'll appreciate the gesture." Jo promised she would be there in the morning, and after disconnecting the call, she scrolled through her phone until she found the pictures of the notebook.

She tapped the screen to enlarge it:

8.17.18 KA $5.00 / $0

8.17.18 BV $5.00 / $0

8.17.18 BV $10.00 / $10.00

8.18.18 SM

8.18.18 OC $20, $20, $20 / $100

Jo studied the jotted notes. "What does this mean?" The dates made sense, but what was KA, BV, SM and OC?

There was also a separate section labeled "Ace" along with dates and dollar amounts. She studied all three of the pictures before finally giving up.

She turned her attention back to the television and began flipping through the channels to see if there was a report on Ashley, but there was nothing.

Jo led Duke down the stairs and outdoors for a quick potty break. She grasped the edge of her pajamas, her eyes drifting to Nash's apartment window. She could see a dim light through the living room shades. She thought about their walk through the gardens.

What would happen to him and Delta if she lost the farm to Miles Parker? The thought caused a cold chill to run down Jo's spine. She couldn't...wouldn't let that happen.

Jo pushed the thought from her mind. "C'mon, Duke. It's time to go in."

Duke scampered up the steps and did a "doggie shake," pelting Jo with droplets of water. "Were you nosing around the bird bath again?" Jo scolded.

Her pooch had the decency to look mildly guilty.

Back in the bedroom, Jo switched off her bedside lamp. She stared into the darkness for a long time. She thought about her parents, about her father and his indiscretions.

Jo had long ago forgiven him. She thought about her mother and those last days, how frail she'd become. Jo could tell from the look in her eyes she'd given up hope of ever being released from prison.

Looking back, it was the turning point for Jessica. The fight was gone; the will to continue living was gone as well.

Jo swiped at the hot tears streaming down the sides of her face. Her mother may have given up, but Joanna Carlton Pepperdine did not intend to do any such thing.

*****

Jo tromped into the kitchen early the next morning and found Delta already up. "You're up early."

"I couldn't sleep. I had one too many troubling thoughts taking up real estate in my mind."

"Mine, too." Jo yawned and quickly covered her mouth. "I'm sorry. I talked to Marlee last night before I went to bed." She told Delta about Ashley Edison's disappearance. "Her car was in the driveway, someone busted down the front door and tore the place apart."

"But no sign of Ashley?" Delta's eyes grew round as saucers.

"Nope."

"Jo." Delta dropped the wooden spoon she was holding. "Janet Ferris and Ashley Edison were neighbors."

"You're kidding."

"She lives in a mobile home outside of town, right down the road from Owen Cole and his family."

"Who is Owen Cole?" Jo asked.

"Owen Cole, the man who was Janet's live-in boyfriend."

Jo planted a palm on her forehead. "Right. But what are the chances the two of them - neighbors - were either murdered or have gone missing?"

"And they worked together," Jo said. "No. I'm going back to my original theory Janet's death ties into the lottery tickets. Someone may have been sneaking around inside the deli. They were looking for something."

"Not to mention it's possible Ashley was a part of the lottery ticket thefts, too."

Jo ran up to her room and returned with her cell phone. "We already know Ace is Ashley."

Delta slipped her reading glasses on and peered through the bottom of the lens as she studied the picture. "Those are for sure dates and dollar amounts, but I don't get the initials." She started to hand the phone to Jo and then snatched it back.

"Wait a minute. Well, if the clue had been any bigger, it would've bitten us right on the end of the nose," Delta said.

"What clue?" Jo asked.

"There. The initials."

"Yes, those are initials," Jo patiently agreed. "But what do they mean?"

"What if the killer's initials are in Janet's notebook?"

"You think KA, BV, SM or OC..." Jo stopped. "OC."

"Owen Cole...those are the initials of Janet's boyfriend."

"Delta, you're a genius. We have Ace, which was Ashley Edison, OC is Owen Cole, now all we have to do is figure out who the other initials belong to." Jo flipped through the pictures, studying the initials in a new light. "KA, BV, SM, OC..." Her heart skipped a beat. "If you're right, if these are the initials of others involved in the lottery ticket thefts, we have a big problem."

"You don't think the SM initials belong to Sherry, do you?"

"I...don't know what to think." Jo's brows furrowed as she studied her phone. "Marlee plans to visit Owen Cole. I'm going with her to take him some food this morning."

"I'm sure Marlee feels terrible," Delta said.

"She does. I still have to wonder." Jo tapped the top of the phone. "Think about it...Janet and Ashley worked together at Four Corners. Not only did they work together they were neighbors. Both may have been involved in a lottery scam. One of them is dead, and the other is missing."

"Since you're going to be in that neck of the woods with Marlee anyway, maybe you can have a look around."

"You mean look around Ashley Edison's place?"

"Well," Delta shrugged. "Maybe Marlee and you could stop by and offer your sympathy to Ashley's family, too."

"Delta." Jo snapped her fingers. "That's a brilliant idea."

Chapter 18

Jo ran upstairs to get ready. By the time she returned downstairs, Sherry was already waiting for her. She decided not to mention her suspicion about the initials, at least not yet.

During the drive to town, the women made small talk, discussing the plans to decorate the bakeshop and mercantile.

They reached the edge of town, and Sherry grew quiet. Jo noticed her clenching her fists. "Is everything all right?"

"Yeah. I was thinking about my future, my plans." Sherry tugged on her seatbelt. "Do you think I'm close to being ready to leave the farm?"

Jo considered the woman's question before answering. "In some ways, I believe you're ready. Working outside the farm is a big step. Marlee is thrilled with your work ethic and enthusiasm. As far as I know, she hasn't received any complaints about you."

"Other than a couple of customers who refused to let me wait on them," Sherry reminded her.

"They don't count. You can't control other people's actions. The only thing you can control is how you react."

"Yeah." Sherry nodded.

"Do *you* think you're getting close to being ready?"

"I'm getting there. Obviously, I'm going to need more than a server's salary to support myself, to pay rent, utilities, groceries, maybe even buy a car."

Jo had kept out of Sherry's business concerning her new job. She knew the woman was depositing almost all of her wages and tips in a bank account but had no idea how much the woman was earning during an average shift. "It depends on what you decide to do and where you decide to live."

"Well, I've been thinking. My father made it clear I'm no longer a part of the family. You're my family - you and the women at *Second Chance*, along with Delta, Nash and Gary."

"So why not consider staying in Divine?" Jo warmed to the idea. "Do you like living here?"

"I love it."

Jo tapped the top of the steering wheel. "One day soon, you and I will spend an afternoon putting together a plan to get you closer to your goal of independence."

Sherry's expression relaxed, and she nodded. "Thanks, Jo. I was hoping you wouldn't mind if I stayed on in Divine after I leave the farm."

"Mind? I'm thrilled you think enough of me and the others to want to stick around."

They turned onto Main Street, and Jo parked in the first empty spot, a few doors down from Marlee's deli. There were only a handful of diners inside, and Jo followed Sherry to the back.

While Sherry headed to the employee breakroom to drop off her things, Jo wandered into the kitchen.

A frantic Marlee darted back and forth. She gave Jo a harried look. "Is it ten-thirty already?"

"Yes, ma'am." Jo took a quick step back, anxious to stay out of the way. "You look busy. Are you sure you still want to make the trip to the Cole residence?"

"Yes, I do. I'm finishing up the meals for Owen. The investigators called me first thing this morning. They plan to stop by here to question the employees again about Janet's death. They claim they have some new information in the case."

"I might have an idea about what they want to discuss."

Marlee dropped some chips inside the to-go bags. "You already talked to the authorities?"

"No." Jo glanced over her shoulder. "It's about the notebook. Delta and I noticed something about the initials. I'm sure the authorities probably noticed it, too."

"You figured out what they mean?"

"Possibly. We can talk while we're in the car. I can drive if you want." Jo jangled her keys.

"Sounds good. I'll tell you how to get there."

Once inside the SUV, Jo shared her theory, how the initials were the initials of some of the others involved in the lottery ticket scheme. "Do you still have the pictures I texted you?"

"I do." Marlee pulled her cell phone from her purse and turned it on before scrolling through the screen. "KA, BV, SM, OC and Ace. Those are the initials you're talking about?"

"Yes. We know 'Ace' is Ashley Edison, who is now missing and there's a possibility of foul play."

"Correct." Marlee shivered. "I can't imagine how terrified she was to have someone break down her door. I wonder how Mary, her mother, is holding up."

"Which brings me to another thought," Jo said, "but don't let me get sidetracked. First, we need to figure out the initials. Could it be these initials belong to some of Janet's co-workers who perhaps unwittingly or even knowingly were involved in the lottery scam?"

"I...suppose." Marlee's eyes narrowed as she studied the screen. "Let's start with the first one, KA. I...my busboy's name is Kevin. Oh my gosh, Jo. Kevin Albright. KA is Kevin Albright."

"What about the next one - BV?"

"BV. I have a server named Brenda, but her last name is Helvinga."

"But BV could be the initials of someone who works at Four Corners."

"True. OC is possibly Owen Cole, Janet's boyfriend," Marlee said. "Last, but not least, is SM."

"Sherry." Jo's jaw tightened. "Sherry Marshall."

Marlee's hand flew to her mouth. "You're right. But there's no number next to the SM initials. The others all have dates and dollar amounts. That one is blank."

"But it's still there," Jo pointed out.

"I don't know what to think." Marlee slid her cell phone back inside her purse. "I guess I'll find out if the authorities suspect the same as we do when they stop by later today."

"I was thinking...what if we stopped by Ashley's place, too? Delta mentioned that she lives in a mobile home with her mother, not far from Cole's house."

"She does." Marlee glanced at the bags of food in the back seat. "I brought plenty of food. We could drop a bag off at Owen Cole's house and another with Ashley's mother, Mary."

After making several turns, the women arrived at the Cole property. As Marlee had previously described, the property consisted of a cluster of mobile homes, arranged in a semi-circle and all connected by a dirt driveway.

Jo cautiously navigated the rutted driveway. She stopped at a mobile home near the center; the one Marlee told her belonged to Owen Cole, Janet's boyfriend. She shifted into park. "Hopefully, he doesn't chase us off his property."

"We'll find out soon enough." Marlee slid out of the vehicle. She opened the back door and grabbed one of the bags of food from the back seat.

Jo waited for her near the front and then the women made their way up the steps, across a wooden deck and to the door.

Marlee rang the bell. When no one answered, she followed up with a light rap.

A dog barked loudly, and finally the door creaked open. A stocky man with dark stubble covering his upper lip and the sides of his face stared out at them. He glanced at the bag of food and then up at the women.

There was a moment of uncomfortable silence before Marlee spoke. "Hello, Mr. Cole. I'm sorry to bother you. I'm Marlee Davison, the owner of *Divine Delicatessen*. I wanted to drop by to let you know how sorry I am about Janet's death and to bring you some food from my deli."

The man grunted and reached for the bag. "What is it?"

"Sandwiches and soup."

"Thank you. I'm working on Janet's memorial. I don't have much money to put into a fancy funeral, so it's going to be a small family gathering day after tomorrow."

"I'm so sorry." Marlee squeezed the palms of her hands together. "This must be a difficult time for you."

"Janet and I were fixin' to get married later this year."

Jo could see the man was visibly upset and her heart went out to him. "I can't believe someone would want to kill her."

"The authorities are working hard on figuring out what happened." Marlee reached out and patted Owen's arm. "In the meantime, if you or your family needs anything, please don't hesitate to give me a call."

"Janet always enjoyed working with you at the deli." He stared at the floor before looking up. "I still can't believe she's gone."

"Neither can I," Marlee said sincerely. "She'll be missed by everyone."

"Thank you for stopping by and for bringing the food."

"You're welcome." Marlee told him again to contact her if he needed anything and the women returned to the vehicle.

Jo pulled the driver's side door shut. "Poor man. You can see he's taking Janet's death hard."

"I feel terrible."

"You can't keep blaming yourself. This has been hard on you, too."

"Yeah." Marlee's lower lip trembled. "It just goes to show no one is promised even one more day."

Jo quoted a familiar Bible verse:

"Why, you do not even know what will happen tomorrow. What is your life? You are a mist that appears for a little while and then vanishes." (James 4:14 NIV)

Marlee dabbed at her eyes. "You're exactly right, which is why we need to make each day count."

Jo steered the SUV back onto the road. "We don't have to stop by Ashley's place if it's going to be too difficult."

"No. I want to. I want the families to know I care about their loved ones and I'm sorry for what happened."

"You had nothing to do with Ashley's disappearance," Jo said.

"Maybe not, but I still feel like there's some sort of connection, some sort of link." Marlee pointed to a mobile home up ahead and on the left. "That's Ashley and her mother's home."

The mobile home, a single wide, was older. The yard was tidy. Like Owen's home, there was a large wooden deck leading to the front entrance.

Lining the deck's railing were several flower boxes, filled with an array of colorful flowers. Jo admired the flowers while Marlee grabbed the second to-go bag from the back seat.

She fell into step as the women made their way to the front door.

"Check it out." Jo pointed to a big gash below a lock and then a shiny new deadbolt directly above it. "This must be where the intruder broke in, right through the front door."

Before they could knock, a woman appeared in the doorway. "Marlee Davison." The woman pushed the screen door open.

"Hello, Mary. I hope we're not bothering you."

"Not at all. Please come in. I saw a vehicle pulling in the drive. I thought it was an unmarked cop car. I'm waiting for the police to stop by with an update on Ashley's disappearance."

Marlee handed the woman the bag of food. "I brought this for you. We just left Owen Cole's place after offering our condolences." She turned to Jo. "This is my friend, Joanna Pepperdine. She owns *Divine Bakeshop* and *Second Chance Mercantile* not far from town."

"You're the lady who opened the halfway house," Mary said.

"Yes, that's me," Jo smiled.

"I've been meaning to get out there. My friend, Norma, said you have some fine stuff for sale and reasonable prices, too."

"I would love for you to stop by sometime."

"I was getting ready to make some tea." The woman carried the bag of food across the living room. "Would you like to join me?"

"Of…" Marlee gave Jo a quick glance, and she shrugged. "Of course. We have a few minutes to spare, but we don't want to trouble you. I'm sure you're not up to having company."

"Company will take my mind off Ashley. I didn't sleep a wink last night, thinking she would walk through the door at any minute." Mary's hand shook as she placed the bag of food on the dining room table.

"I'm sorry, Mary. I wish there was something we could do to help."

The dining room was open to the other end of the trailer, and Mary continued to the galley kitchen. "Only the Good Lord can help now. He knows where my Ashley is, and I've been praying hard that she'll be found safe."

"Has she ever gone missing before?" Jo asked.

"There was one time, a couple of years ago, she took off. We got into an argument, and she threatened to move out. This time is different." Mary filled the kettle with water and set it on top of the stove. "You said you stopped by the Cole place down the road and talked to Owen?"

"Yes. We just left there," Jo said.

"Owen didn't meet you at the door with a shotgun?"

"No." Marlee shook her head. "We talked for a couple of minutes. He's taking Janet's death hard."

"I'm sure he is. He's also taking it out on me."

Chapter 19

Jo stared at Mary. "Janet's boyfriend is blaming you for her death?"

"I'm sure by now you heard about the lottery ticket investigation," Mary said.

"We have. According to the authorities, Ashley and Janet were 'borrowing' tickets from *Four Corners Mini-Mart* and scratching them off. When they hit a fairly good jackpot, they would replace the money."

"That about sums it up. Before Ashley went missing, we talked about the lottery tickets."

Jo leaned in, eager to find out what Ashley had said.

"She claims Janet was the one who first approached her with the idea of taking the tickets and scratching them in the hopes of hitting the big one."

"But wouldn't the store manager cancel the tickets when they found out they were stolen?" Jo asked.

"Yes, except Ashley was managing the store when Janet borrowed the tickets. There was no video surveillance of the thefts. The missing tickets were never reported and the tickets were never canceled." Mary explained the women's scheme had held up so far, and they were able to turn in the winning tickets to cover the discrepancies.

Jo thought about the notebook. "We found a notebook with Ashley's nickname along with some dates, initials and dollar amounts inside Janet's locker."

Mary carried the teacups to the table. "This is the first I've heard about a notebook."

"The police didn't mention it to you?" Marlee asked.

"Nope. Not a peep."

"Thank you." Jo took the cup from Mary as she mulled over the cryptic notebook. Perhaps she was way off track, and the notebook was unrelated to Janet's death and Ashley's disappearance. She remembered the front door. "I see you have a new lock on your front door."

"Yes. I just installed it. That's where the intruder busted in. I knew as soon as I came home yesterday something was terribly wrong." Mary told them her first clue was Ashley's car parked in the driveway. "I was surprised she was home. When I got to the door and saw it wide open, I knew something had happened to Ashley."

Mary's eyes filled with tears, and Marlee reached for her hand. "We can talk about something else."

"Yes." Mary nodded. "Perhaps we should."

The women made small talk, and after finishing their tea, Marlee stood. "I better get back to the deli before the lunch crowd hits."

Mary walked them to the door. "I called all of Ashley's friends...anyone who I thought might know what happened to her."

Jo followed Marlee onto the deck. "Was anything missing from the house, other than Ashley?"

"Ashley's purse and all of her identification."

"Is her cell phone missing, too?"

"It is. The investigators were putting a tracer on it. I left a message for Deputy Franklin to see if he found anything yet, but I haven't heard back."

"I'll be praying for her," Jo said.

"Thank you. I hope they find her soon."

"You let me know if you need anything, Mary." Marlee gave her a gentle hug, and then the women returned to the SUV.

Mary stood on the deck watching them back out of the driveway before returning inside.

"Something doesn't sound right," Jo said. "Do you think Ashley murdered Janet and then made it look like an intruder broke in?"

"It is odd that her purse, her cell phone and all of her identification are gone, too. Why would an intruder take her identification?"

"Unless they planned to force her to withdraw money from her bank accounts, which means the authorities would have a trail if the kidnapper or even Ashley tried to take money out, they would easily be able to track it."

"True," Marlee said. "So we're back to square one with the notebook, if what Mary said was true and Ashley and Janet were the only two involved in the lottery ticket thefts."

When they reached the deli, Jo pulled around back to let Marlee out.

"Thanks for driving and for tagging along."

"You're welcome. Thank you for letting me. Tell Sherry I'll be back later."

"Will do." Marlee gave Jo a thumbs up and hurried inside the deli.

Back at the farm, Jo dropped her purse and keys inside. Delta was nowhere in sight, but there were several pans of brownies cooling on the counter. She checked the house and then headed to the bakeshop where she found Delta behind the counter.

"What are you doing?" Jo asked.

"Raylene is feeling under the weather. I told her to go rest, and I would cover for her."

"I can handle this." Jo joined her friend behind the counter.

"How did Owen Cole's visit go?"

"It was sad. Owen is taking Janet's death hard. He didn't seem to have any ill will toward Marlee, and I know she's relieved. We also stopped by Ashley Edison's place and talked to her mother, Mary." Jo briefly explained how Ashley had confessed to her mother about the lottery ticket scheme. "Mary claims she knew nothing about a notebook and the lottery scheme involved just Janet and Ashley."

"So maybe the notebook isn't related to Janet's murder."

"I don't know...unless Ashley didn't tell her mother that part. Mary said the intruder came in through the front door and tore the place apart. Ashley, along with her cell phone and purse, are missing."

"What if she staged her own disappearance?" Delta asked.

"I thought the same thing. If so, the authorities will be able to locate her or whoever has her cell phone and if she uses her credit or debit cards."

A couple entered the bakeshop and Delta made her way out.

The next couple of hours were busy as Jo waited on customers. After her shift ended, she walked to the back to Raylene's apartment. She knocked lightly, and the door opened moments later.

A pale Raylene appeared in the doorway.

"Delta said you weren't feeling well."

"I have a headache." Raylene pressed a light hand to her forehead. "It's starting to ease up a little. I feel bad about not being able to finish my shift."

"Delta and I covered it. Have you eaten anything today?"

"Not since early this morning. Thinking about food makes me sick to my stomach."

"You should try to eat something. I'm going to see if Delta has a remedy for a migraine."

Raylene told her she was going to lie back down but would leave her door unlocked.

Jo found her friend in the kitchen. "Raylene hasn't eaten anything since this morning. I wonder if there's something she could try that might help her headache."

"Nuts, bananas, avocadoes. We have all of those."

"I'll fix Raylene a plate." Jo assembled a plate of the suggested foods and returned to the woman's apartment. The lights were off. She tiptoed inside and quietly placed the plate on the dresser before making her way back out.

"Did you get her to eat?" Delta asked when Jo returned.

"She was resting, so I set the plate next to her bed."

"I was gonna have you leave a couple of Advil along with the other stuff, but I see we're out."

"I can swing by Four Corners when I pick Sherry up," Jo said.

"Get a couple of bottles," Delta shoved her hand on her hip. "Any word from Miles Parker?"

"Nope." Jo shook her head. "Maybe he found out Chris is my attorney and was investigating his claim, he panicked and decided to drop it."

"That may be wishful thinking."

"I know. The hardest part is waiting to see what the man is going to do next."

Delta asked Jo to deliver the freshly baked brownies to the bakeshop. After dropping them off, she returned to the house where the queen of the kitchen insisted she didn't need any help.

Soon, it would be time to pick Sherry up at the deli. "I think I'll run by Claire's place." Jo was in the process of renovating her attic. Nash had already installed new light fixtures, along with sheets of drywall. If all went as planned, her cozy book nook would be ready in time for the long winter months.

She still needed to decorate the nook and decided *Claire's Collectibles* would be the perfect place to start searching for the furnishings.

"You gonna ask her what she knows about Janet's death and Ashley's disappearance?" Delta asked.

"Yes. Claire has lived in Divine for decades. She's in a prime spot to hear the chit chat around town. She may have heard something."

"You want some company?"

Jo pointed to the mixing bowl. "You're up to your elbows in frosting."

"I wasn't talking about me. I was thinking about maybe seeing if you wanted to invite one of the gals to go with you."

"Which would be perfect if not for Raylene not feeling well and Sherry in town working. The only other one who might be able to go is Leah. I think she's working with Nash today."

"Leah hasn't been out much lately," Delta said. "Wouldn't hurt for you to invite her to tag along."

"You're right." Jo thanked Delta for the idea, grabbed her purse and headed to Nash's workshop.

She stepped inside. The smell of varnish permeated the air. She let out a small cough and waved a hand in front of her face. "My goodness, those are some powerful fumes."

Leah swiveled on the barstool, paintbrush in hand. "It is a little strong."

A floor fan struggled to keep the air inside the workshop circulating, but the small fan was no match for the overpowering fumes.

"I was getting ready to open the overhead door." Nash set his brush on the rim of his can. "So what brings you to my neck of the woods?"

"I stopped by to see if Leah would like to ride into town with me to pick up Sherry. I plan to swing by Claire's place first."

"Sounds good to me. Leah and I could use a break from these fumes," Nash said.

"I would love to go." Leah placed her paintbrush in a plastic bag and hopped off the stool. "I'll change and be right back." She hurried out of the workshop and Nash turned to Jo. "Looking for treasures to add to the attic?"

"I am. My awesome and amazing right-hand man will soon be finished with my latest project."

"Your wish is my command," Nash teased. He grew sober. "Who was the man you brought by yesterday? I take it he's not a local."

Jo knew Nash was talking about Chris. "Chris Nyles. He's a friend. He's also my attorney."

Nash raised a brow. "Is everything all right?"

"I hope so." Jo shifted uneasily, anxious to avoid discussing Miles Parker and her possible predicament. "He's helping me out with a small issue."

"I figured he was more than just an acquaintance. You two seemed pretty familiar with one another."

Jo detected a hint of something in Nash's voice. Whatever it may have been, it was quickly gone. "I planned to start mudding the drywall in the attic first thing tomorrow morning."

"Perfect," Jo beamed.

"It will be kind of early."

"You won't bother me." The attic door was not far from Jo's master bedroom door, and the stairs leading to the third floor ran along one of her bedroom walls. "I'll make sure I'm presentable. What time do you think you're going to start?"

"Would seven be too early?"

"Not at all. In fact, why don't you let me help? Delta doesn't like me in the kitchen in the mornings."

"Sure."

"I'll bring the coffee and the donuts," Jo joked.

Leah returned, and Jo glanced at her watch. "We better get going."

The ride to town flew by as Jo's resident chattered nonstop. All it took was asking Leah what her plans were after she left the farm.

"Oh, I would love to own a farm of my own. I want it to be sustainable, producing organic fruits and vegetables, and implementing green practices."

Leah rattled on about not only leaving a small footprint but also living as close to "off the grid" as possible.

"You've given this some thought. I admire you for looking ahead."

When they arrived in town, they drove past the deli, parking in front of *Claire's Coin Laundromat*. The women exited the vehicle. They strolled past the laundromat and stopped when they reached the antique shop.

Jo waited for Leah to step inside. The fragrant aroma of pine mingled with cinnamon greeted them.

The doorbell chimed, announcing their arrival and Claire emerged from the back. "Hello, ladies."

"Hi, Claire." Jo gave her friend a quick hug. "I stopped by to see what treasures you have in stock that might work in my future book nook."

"You came to the right place. I have lots of great stuff." Claire changed the subject. "I was down at

Marlee's earlier eating lunch, and one of your lovely ladies from the farm waited on me. At first, I didn't recognize her."

"Sherry," Jo said. "Marlee just hired her on a trial basis at least until after the fall festival."

"She's doing a fine job," Claire said. "I heard about Janet Ferris' death. I couldn't believe it when I heard someone strangled her out behind the deli."

"It's terrible. We all need to be careful until the authorities can figure out who murdered her."

"And now Ashley Edison is missing." Claire tsk-tsked. "Poor Mary must be beside herself."

"Marlee and I visited Mary earlier. She's in shock."

"Ashley has given her mother more than her share of gray hairs," Claire said. "The authorities were in here earlier, questioning me about anything I may have noticed around the time of Janet's death."

"And did you notice anything?"

"Well, at first I didn't think so, but the more I thought about it something odd did happen the day before Janet's death."

Chapter 20

Instead of telling Jo what happened, Claire motioned for Leah and her to follow behind to the back of the store, along a short hall and then to another door that led to the alley.

"Is there someone watching the store?" Jo asked.

"Nah." Claire waved dismissively. "It'll be fine. Even if someone comes in, we'll be right back."

"You're trusting," Leah said.

"Honey, this is Divine. No one is going to mess with the store."

They traipsed across a cement block patio, riddled with weeds dotting the gaps in the blocks.

"No, they're going to start killing people instead," Jo said.

"True." Claire stopped when they reached the wooden fence and a row of metal garbage cans. "I was emptying my trash the other day and noticed a bunch of scratch-off tickets someone had tossed on top. At first, I didn't think too much about it. You know sometimes kids come back here and start messing around."

"Until the police showed up and you found out about Ashley and Janet's lottery scheme."

"Yep." Claire pointed down the alley. "Notice how the deli is a straight shot from here? I think the tickets I found in this can are somehow related to Janet's scratch-offs. It's too coincidental."

Jo studied the distance between the two buildings. "So it could be that someone sneaked into the deli and also dumped a stack of scratched tickets here."

"That's what I'm thinkin'," Claire said. "Maybe it was Ashley, getting rid of some of the evidence before trying to get into Janet's locker."

"Looking for the notebook," Jo said.

"Right."

"There's one big problem. I'm not sure how the notebook ties into this whole lottery ticket scheme. According to Mary, the only two involved were Janet and Ashley."

"I haven't seen the notebook," Claire said. "Marlee mentioned you took some pictures of it before she turned it over to the investigators, but I didn't have time to check it out."

"I can show them to you." Jo whipped her cell phone out of her back pocket. She turned it on and scrolled through the screen until she found the pictures.

Claire tapped the screen to enlarge the picture before popping her reading glasses off her head and onto her nose. "It certainly appears to be dates, followed by initials and then dollar amounts. Ace is Ashley Edison."

"Correct."

"Well, it stands to reason the others are individuals' initials. Perhaps there were others involved, and Ashley just didn't tell her mother. KA could be Kevin Albright, Marlee's busboy. BV, I don't know. OC, those are Owen's initials...Janet's boyfriend and the last SM, I'm not sure." Claire handed the cell phone back. "The authorities confiscated the tickets as potential evidence."

Leah, who had so far remained silent, spoke. "SM. Those are Sherry's initials. Sherry Marshall."

"Oh, dear." Claire frowned. "You don't think your Sherry was involved, do you?"

"No, but why would the initials of the deli employees be written inside a cryptic notebook kept by a woman who is now dead?" Jo asked. "If they weren't involved in the lottery ticket scheme, why was Janet keeping a notebook?"

"We may never know," Claire said.

The trio returned to the antique shop where Jo wandered up and down the aisles, searching for furniture for her book nook. She found a set of antique bookcases in a shade of golden oak, a perfect match to her wood floors. "I'll take both of the bookcases."

"They're lovely antique pieces." Claire reached for her receipt pad. She quoted Jo a fair price and Jo handed her a debit card. "I'll ask Nash to stop by and pick them up the next time he's in town."

"I'll have them wrapped and ready." Claire scanned Jo's card and handed it back to her. "I found something interesting about Ashley's disappearance."

"What is that?" Jo shoved the receipt in her purse.

"Well, Mary is retired. She doesn't get out much anymore because she doesn't drive."

"Ashley chauffeured her mother around," Jo guessed.

"Except for Thursdays," Claire said. "Mary and a friend head to Centerpoint Junction every Thursday for weekly bingo games at the VFW Hall."

"Which is the same day Ashley went missing," Jo said. "Either someone knew Mary's schedule and waited until they knew Ashley would be home and alone or Ashley waited for her mom to leave and then staged her own disappearance."

"But how did she go into hiding?" Leah asked. "She would need someone to help her disappear since she left her car behind."

"That, my dear, is the million dollar question."

Jo thanked Claire for the information and promised Nash would stop by in the next day or so to pick up the bookcases.

Leah and Jo strolled down the sidewalk to the deli where they spotted Sherry waiting for them near the front window.

Jo waved, and they headed inside. "Are you ready to go home?"

"Yes. My feet are killing me. We were super busy today. This place was a madhouse."

"Is Marlee here?"

"She's out back," Sherry said.

"I want to chat with her," Jo said. "Do you mind hanging out for a few minutes?"

"Of course not."

Jo traipsed through the server area and then the kitchen before stepping onto the back patio. Her eyes were drawn to Claire's fence a short distance away. Something told her that whoever had been inside Marlee's place had also dumped the lottery tickets in Claire's trash, believing no one would be the wiser.

She nearly collided with Marlee as she rounded the side of the building.

"Whoops!"

Jo jumped back. "Sorry, Marlee."

"It's okay." She pressed a hand to her chest. "I'm just a little jittery."

"You're not the only one. Claire told me she found some discarded scratch-offs in her trash bin."

"Yes. The investigators were here earlier, asking more questions and searching the place again. I asked them about Ashley's disappearance and if they thought there was a connection between Janet's death and Ashley's disappearance."

"What did they say?"

"I got the standard answer. They are still investigating, both are open cases and they can't comment." Marlee lowered her voice. "I did find out Ashley's cell phone is turned off. So far, there's been no activity on her credit or debit cards."

"I feel sorry for Mary," Jo said.

"Yes, poor thing."

"What are you doing?" Jo pointed to the hammer her friend was holding.

"Making sure all of the locks and windows are secure."

Marlee told Jo the authorities questioned her about the notebook, confirming their suspicion the initials in the book were somehow associated with the scratch-off scheme.

"Which puts Sherry back on the list of suspects...SM."

"Right. They talked to Sherry, along with my busboy, Kevin, and Brenda. Don't worry...I was there the entire time."

"Who is Brenda?"

"Brenda Helvinga - or should I say Brenda Helvinga-Visser."

"So she's the BV in the notebook."

"My guess is yes," Marlee said. "Although Brenda, Kevin and of course, Sherry, swear they knew nothing about Janet's ticket theft, other than seeing her scratching tickets on her breaks." She changed the subject. "You got a minute?"

"Sure. Leah rode into town with me. She and Sherry are out front waiting."

"Because of Janet's death and now Ashley's disappearance, not to mention someone snooping around inside the deli, I wanted to take another quick look upstairs to make sure it's secure."

"Did the police already look up there?"

"No. I checked the other day, after Janet's death. I told the investigators the lock was still in place."

"How do you get there?" Jo asked.

"The only entrance is at the top of these steps." Marlee nodded toward the side of the building where a steep set of steps led to the second level. "Right now, I'm using it for storage. The deli was originally the town's hotel, restaurant and saloon."

Marlee began climbing the steps, and Jo followed her. "At one time, there was a set of interior steps leading to the second floor, but the previous owner walled it off."

When they reached the top of the stairs, Marlee pulled a set of keys from her pocket and unlocked the door.

The door opened to a spacious foyer. There were two sets of doors on each side and a fifth door on the opposite end.

Marlee opened the first door on the right. She stepped to the side while Jo peered into the large open space.

"Do you have plans for the upstairs?"

"I do. I was thinking of turning it into rental units. I think I could get a few hundred bucks a month in rent. There's enough room to build at least a couple of apartments."

"Very cool," Jo was impressed. "You could make a tidy sum every month if you took the time to renovate."

"That's my plan." Marlee took a quick look around before joining Jo in the hall.

The women inspected the other empty rooms and began heading out when Jo pointed to a small door near the exit.

"What's in there?"

"It's a storage closet." Marlee grasped the knob and pulled. The door refused to budge. "This door is a little sticky." She gave it a good yank, and the door flew open.

"What a mess." Marlee shook her head at the clutter inside. "I might as well grab the spare vacuum while I'm up here. The one downstairs is on the fritz." She eased the vacuum from the closet and a plastic bag fell to the floor.

Jo snatched the bag off the floor and handed it to her friend.

"What's this?" Marlee grabbed the bag and peered inside. "There's something in here." She tipped it over and dumped the contents onto the floor.

Jo's hand flew to her mouth. "Oh my gosh."

Chapter 21

"I think we found out why someone keeps trying to break into your deli." Jo picked up a stack of unscratched lottery tickets. "These are ten-dollar tickets."

Marlee picked up another stack. "These are twenty-dollar tickets. There are hundreds of dollars in tickets."

"There's something else." Marlee picked up a thick wad of cash and fanned the bills. "Janet. Janet must have hidden the bag in the closet. No wonder she was always offering to come up here."

"You gave her a key."

"She borrowed the key. Now that I think about it, she forgot to return it a couple of months ago, and I had to remind her."

"Which means she could have easily made a copy," Jo said. "What about the deli? Did she have a key to the lower level and restaurant?"

"No. I don't give keys to the servers or busboys. The upstairs key is different from the one for the main part of the building. I figured there was no sense in installing new locks up here since I plan on renovating the place in the near future," Marlee said. "I still don't get why Janet would hide these tickets upstairs."

"Maybe she took them during her shift at the mini-mart and didn't have time to drop them off at home before covering a shift at the deli, so she hid them up here and planned to pick them up later," Jo theorized.

"The killer...the killer is after these tickets." Marlee waved the stack of scratch-offs she was holding. "Whoever has been messing around my place - they're after these tickets and money."

"And they'll probably be back again." Jo returned to the entrance and knelt down to inspect the lock.

"There's no sign of forced entry, so perhaps they haven't thought to look up here yet."

"I need to let Detective Beck, the man in charge, know what's going on." Marlee placed the tickets and cash back into the bag. She shoved the bag to the back of the closet. "I'm going to leave this right here, right where we found it."

Marlee locked the door behind them, and the women descended the steps. "I'm going to call him right now."

"What if one of your employees is the one searching for the tickets and cash? I wouldn't make the call in a place where someone might be able to listen in."

"True. Let me grab my cell phone and the detective's card." Marlee dashed inside, returning moments later with her cell phone. She dialed the number on the card and asked to speak to the detective. "I see. Yes, I understand. And when is he returning?" There was a moment of silence. "Is there anyone else handling the Janet Ferris investigation? Yes, I would like to leave a message."

Marlee cupped her hand over the phone. "The detective is in court today. I'm leaving a message for someone I've never heard of before." She left a brief message, telling the person she had an important matter to discuss and then rattled off her cell phone number before disconnecting the call. "I don't know if leaving a message is going to help."

"Why?"

"They transferred me to someone else, to someone who knows nothing about Janet's case." Marlee lifted her gaze, warily eyeing the stairs. "What are we going to do?"

"I don't know. Pray that the man covering for Detective Beck returns your call."

Marlee consulted her watch. "I better get back to work."

Jo met Sherry and Leah near the front of the deli and the trio headed to the vehicle. "I need to make a quick stop at the mini-mart."

She pulled into Four Corners and parked near the front of the building. "I'll be right back."

"I'll go with you," Sherry said. "I want to pick up a Diet Coke." She turned to Leah. "Would you like anything? My treat."

"Sure. I'll take a regular Coke," Leah said. "Thanks."

"You're welcome."

Jo left the vehicle running and joined Sherry near the mini-mart's entrance. "That was very thoughtful, Sherry."

"Claire, your friend from the antique store down the street, stopped by for lunch. She left me a generous tip."

"I heard you waited on her earlier. She said you did an excellent job," Jo said.

The women wandered up and down the aisles until they found the small section of over-the-counter medicines.

Jo picked up a bottle of Advil. "Six dollars for twenty tablets? That's highway robbery."

"The price does seem steep. Maybe you should wait and buy them in Centerpoint Junction."

"Raylene isn't feeling well, and we're out of pain reliever. I'll get these and grab a bigger bottle on our next shopping trip."

Jo followed Sherry to the coolers and watched as she grabbed several cans of soda. "I figured maybe the others would like a Coke or Diet Coke, too."

"I'm sure they will." Jo paid for her purchase first and then stood off to the side as Sherry paid for her items. While she waited, she perused the display of lottery tickets, remembering the tickets Marlee and she had found inside the upstairs closet.

The tickets all looked familiar. There was only one roll of twenty-dollar tickets. The clerk counted out Sherry's change and stepped over to the lottery display case. "Would you like to buy some scratch-offs?"

"No." Jo wrinkled her nose. "I'm not much of a gambler." She tapped the Plexiglas and pointed to the roll of twenty-dollar tickets. "Do you sell many of the *Kansas Riches* tickets?"

"You would think at that price we wouldn't sell many, but these are flying off the rack. They're brand new tickets. We just got them in yesterday morning."

"You're saying you just got these tickets in yesterday morning?" Jo studied the ticket, no longer certain that it was the one Marlee and she had found in the bag.

"Right." The woman nodded. "I know for a fact because I'm the one who put them on the display wheel."

"Are there any other twenty-dollar tickets?" Jo asked.

"Nope. We were getting low on inventory and sold out of the higher priced scratch-offs and the dollar ones until these came in."

"I see. Thank you." Jo slowly exited the store, her mind whirling. If what the clerk said was true, that the tickets were new and put out *after* Janet's death, then someone else put the plastic bag containing the scratch-off tickets and cash in the deli's upstairs closet.

She waited until Sherry and she were back in the SUV. "I need to check on something real quick at the deli. Do you mind if we go back for a couple of minutes?"

"Nope. We're just along for the ride," Leah quipped.

Jo returned to the deli. "I'll be back in a jiffy." She darted inside and made a beeline for the back where she found Marlee standing in front of the fryer. "Hey, Marlee."

Marlee did a double take when she saw Jo. "I thought you were gone."

"I was. I had to stop at Four Corners to pick up some Advil. While I was there, I was checking out the lottery tickets and discovered something very interesting." Jo briefly explained how the clerk had told her they sold out of the twenty-dollar tickets and had just gotten in a new batch.

"Janet and Ashley probably stole them all," Marlee said.

"Maybe. Do you remember the name of the twenty-dollar scratch-offs?"

"I think it was riches something."

"*Kansas Riches*?" Jo asked.

"I think so."

"Then there's no way Janet stashed those tickets in the upstairs closet. Can I take a quick look inside the bag again?"

"I'll do one better. Carlos, my cook, should be back from his break any moment. I'll go with you."

Jo returned to the SUV to let the women know she would be a few more minutes. "Marlee is checking on something for me, but she has to wait for her cook to return."

"Carlos," Sherry said.

"Yeah. He's on break."

The women told her to take her time, and Jo returned to the kitchen where she found Marlee talking to the dark-haired man she'd previously met.

"Hello, Carlos."

"Hello, Ms. Pepperdine."

"I have to get something for Jo," Marlee said. "I'll be right back."

The women exited through the back door and climbed the stairs to the second floor.

"Have you heard back from the detective filling in?" Jo asked.

"Yes. I missed his call. I was waiting tables in the front and had left my cell phone in the back. I called back as soon as I realized who it was, but now we're playing phone tag. It's frustrating, to say the least."

She finished unlocking the door and made a beeline for the closet. Marlee picked up the bag and pulled out a handful of the tickets.

"Those aren't it. I'm looking for the twenty-dollar tickets," Jo said.

"They're in here somewhere." Marlee reached into the bag a second time and pulled out another handful.

"There." Jo pointed to a larger ticket in the middle of the stack. "I think the bigger tickets are the more expensive ones."

Marlee flipped the ticket over. "Well, will you look at that?"

Chapter 22

Jo's heart skipped a beat as she stared at the *Kansas Riches* scratch-off. "This...this means Janet wasn't the one who hid this bag of tickets and cash. It had to be someone else."

"Someone has a key to the upstairs, but who?"

"It must be an employee."

"So I have an employee who is not only a thief but also a killer." Marlee briefly closed her eyes. "What am I going to do?"

"We can't panic, at least not yet." Jo studied the hallway. "Do you have your cell phone on you?"

"Yes." Marlee showed Jo her phone. "I'm keeping it with me until I talk to the detective."

"I'm sure he'll call you back. All you need to do is explain you believe someone may have tried to break-in and then tell him you believe whoever it is, is after these tickets and cash."

"Which means there are two people," Marlee said.

Jo flipped through the tickets as she attempted to put the pieces together. "You're right. Someone hid this bag of tickets and cash in the closet after Janet's death."

"And someone else is desperate to get their hands on them. It has to be two people." Marlee carefully placed the tickets back inside the closet. "It's three o'clock."

"So we have the rest of the afternoon to wait for the authorities to contact you again and let them know there might be more than one person involved."

*****

Jo dropped the women off in front of the mercantile before parking next to the house. She took the back steps two at a time, making her way inside.

The tantalizing aroma of garlic and cilantro lingered in the air. Delta was MIA.

She passed through the dining room when she heard the sound of Delta's laughter coming from the front porch.

Jo changed directions and tiptoed to the doorway where she noticed Delta and Gary cozying up on the porch swing. She reached for the handle and then changed her mind.

With a small smile on her face, Jo began humming as she climbed the stairs. She dropped her purse off in her room before returning downstairs.

Jo drifted to the doorway. Gary and Delta were still sitting on the swing. Not wanting to disturb them, she headed out through the back door with the bottle of Advil in hand.

Raylene's apartment was empty and her bed made. The plate of food Jo had dropped off earlier was gone.

Jo's next stop was the bakeshop where she found Raylene standing behind the counter. "How are you feeling?"

"Much better. I ate some of the food you left." Raylene smiled.

"I brought you some Advil." Jo held up the bottle of pills. "Would you like to take a couple?"

"Yes, please."

"I can take over while you grab a glass of water."

"Sherry picked up some sodas when she was in town." Raylene popped two pills in her mouth and took a big swig of soda.

"Let me know if you need a couple more before you go to bed." Jo turned to go, and Raylene stopped her.

"Hey...did you see Delta and Gary on the porch?"

"Yes. They look rather...cozy," Jo said. She remembered Nash telling her how Gary had asked him for advice on asking Delta out on a date.

"I think they're cute together." Raylene scrunched her nose.

"I do, too, but don't go teasing Delta about it," Jo warned.

"Oh, believe me, I would never do that."

Jo wandered from the bakeshop to the mercantile. She stopped to inspect the wheelbarrow displays and noticed the bushel baskets were half-full.

The mercantile was bustling with shoppers, and Jo made her rounds, assisting customers who needed help. She stopped by the cash register where Kelli was working. "How are sales?"

"Brisk. I've been meaning to tell you we're getting a lot of shoppers asking about souvenirs."

"Souvenirs?"

"You know...the middle-of-nowhere tourist souvenirs."

"I hadn't thought of that." Jo had no idea what type of souvenirs would appeal to tourists, considering there wasn't much to the area's main attraction - the center point of the contiguous United States.

"I was thinking..." Kelli's voice trailed off.

"Yes."

Kelli began fiddling with the pen she was holding. "I've been doing a little research and looking up crafty stuff online."

"You have an idea?"

"Yes. I mean, it's probably silly and nothing that would actually sell."

"Now that's where you're wrong. I don't think any idea is silly. I would love to hear your thoughts."

Kelli brightened. "I found some colored pencils and made some sketches. They're just rough ideas."

She reached behind the counter and pulled out several sheets of paper. "I've been working on them during my breaks when business is slow."

"Let's see what you have." Jo eased in next to her.

"This is one of my favorites." Kelli handed Jo a sketch of sunflowers, their centers tilted toward bright beams of sunlight, with rolling green fields as the backdrop.

"This is very, very good." The woman's artistic talents impressed Jo. "What were you thinking?"

"We could sell magnets, maybe even bookmarks, something with the Divine name on it."

"I think it's a great idea." Jo handed the sketch back. "Would you like to do a little more research, maybe find some online companies who could create a few samples using your sketches?"

"I...actually already have," Kelli said. "There's a company in Wichita that might be able to help us."

"Then let's move forward. Let's order some samples and go from there," Jo said. "I like the idea of the bookmarks and magnets, perhaps even some pens."

"Right," Kelli beamed. "Thanks, Jo."

"*Thank you* for suggesting it."

Kelli promised to get things rolling, and then meet with Jo for final approval and ordering the samples.

By the time Jo exited the stores, the front porch swing was empty and Gary's pickup truck, which had been parked next to the toolshed, was gone. She could hear Delta singing as soon as she stepped inside the house. "There you are."

"There I am? I was beginning to wonder what happened to you." Delta reached into the cabinet and pulled out a large stainless steel pot. "How is Claire?"

"Claire is fine. We had a nice chat. I bought two antique bookcases for my book nook." Jo made a mental note to ask Nash to stop by to pick them up on his next trip to town. "While I was there, Claire told me she found some scratch-off tickets in her trashcan out back."

"Janet was dumping her discarded tickets in Claire's trash?"

"Maybe. There's something else." Jo told her how Marlee and she had gone upstairs to have a look around. "We found a bag of tickets and cash stashed in an upstairs storage closet."

"Janet hid them in there?"

"That's what we initially thought, until I discovered at least one of the stacks of tickets wasn't available for sale until yesterday."

"So the tickets didn't belong to Janet," Delta said.

"Correct."

"How did the tickets and cash get into the deli's upstairs closet?"

"Someone has a key, maybe an employee." Jo rubbed her chin. "Ashley is missing, which means someone else hid the tickets in the closet."

"Then why was someone trying to get into the employee lockers?"

"That's a good question, and I wish I knew the answer. It appears there may be two accomplices or even killers/kidnappers on the loose. Someone is hiding tickets and cash, and someone is looking for them."

Delta folded her arms. "And it sounds as if the one who is hiding the tickets and cash is also employed by Marlee."

"It stands to reason."

"Marlee needs to let the authorities know what's going on."

"She has. Unfortunately, the detective handling the case is in court today. Marlee left a message for the man who's filling in for him. He called her back, she missed the call and now they're playing phone tag."

"What's she gonna do?" Delta asked.

"I don't know. I have a feeling whoever left those tickets and the money...or whoever is looking for them will be back tonight." Jo studied her cell phone and the photographs of Janet's notebook.

There was a small noise near the kitchen door, and Jo turned to see Raylene standing in the doorway. "Hello, Raylene. You look like you're feeling a little better."

"I am. The Advil took care of what little headache I had left." Raylene stepped into the kitchen. "Sherry and I were talking about the dead co-worker, Janet, and how the assistant store manager is missing. They were involved in some sort of lottery ticket scheme."

"Yes." Jo briefly explained what had transpired.

"Is it possible the woman, Ashley, staged her own disappearance?" Raylene asked. "Think about it...she just happened to be home alone, yet her purse is missing, and as far as you know, she hasn't used her credit cards or cell phone."

"Which means she has an accomplice, but who?" Jo stared at Raylene thoughtfully. "You know what? If Ashley has gone into hiding, I think I have an idea about who is helping her out. And I'm thinking a quick trip to town might confirm my suspicions."

Chapter 23

"I'll go with you," Raylene offered.

"Are you sure?" Jo studied the woman's face. "You still look a little under the weather."

"Like I said, I'm feeling much better. Besides, some fresh air will do me good." Raylene waited by the back door while Jo grabbed her keys. "I'm curious about the notebook you found."

"We originally thought whoever sneaked in the deli the other night was after the notebook, but now we're beginning to think they were after the cash and tickets. Marlee surprised them, and they took off. The notebook may be a clue, but we're not sure how it fits in with Janet's death."

"It's a shame I can't take a look at it," Raylene said.

"You can, at least you can look at the pictures." After they were inside the vehicle, Jo handed Raylene her purse. "They're on my cell phone in the side pocket of my purse."

"I found them." Raylene grew quiet as she studied the screen. "I need to get the whole picture. Ashley, *Four Corners Mini-Mart's* assistant manager, and Janet, a server at *Divine Delicatessen* and a part-time employee at the mini-mart, were stealing scratch-off lottery tickets. The store manager discovered a discrepancy in the ticket inventory and started to investigate. Janet, figuring she would be a suspect, decided to quit. During her work break at the deli, she made some sort of scene inside the mini-mart. She drove back to the deli and later that day she was found strangled inside her car."

"Yes," Jo said. "Not long after, Marlee discovered the deli's back door was ajar. We think someone may have been trying to get inside Janet's locker because it looked like someone had tried to pry the lockers open."

"To search for the notebook...you think."

"Possibly. But now we found the tickets and cash...the person or persons may have been after those instead."

"Could be," Raylene agreed. "So Janet is murdered and then Ashley Edison, the mini-mart's assistant manager and lottery ticket accomplice, goes missing."

"In a nutshell," Jo said.

"These look like initials. Who is Ace?"

"Ashley Edison. KA is Kevin something, the busboy. BV is Brenda Visser, another server."

"Sherry's initials are SM," Raylene said. "You don't think Sherry was involved in the ticket thefts, do you?"

"No. The scheme was in the works long before Sherry started working there."

"So there's a good chance whoever murdered Janet is an employee at the deli or the mini-mart," Raylene said.

"Correct."

"We're going to the deli?"

"No. We're going to the hardware store," Jo said. "I think there's more to Ashley Edison's disappearance than meets the eye."

Jo gave Raylene the option of waiting in the vehicle but Raylene, curious to find out what lead Jo was working on, followed her inside.

Wayne Malton, the owner of *Tool Time Hardware* was nowhere in sight. Charlotte, Wayne's wife, was behind the counter. "Joanna, it's so nice to see you again."

"It's nice to see you, too." Jo glanced around the store. "Is Wayne taking the day off?"

"No. He's in the back helping a customer load some bags of mulch. Is there something I can help you with?"

"Maybe. I'm looking for your door locks, specifically the deadbolt kind, one that would work on an exterior door."

"We have a few in stock." Charlotte led the women to an aisle near the front. "This is all we have."

Jo inspected the locks. Her heart skipped a beat when she spied a lock identical to the one on Mary Edison's front door. She removed it from the rack. "Do you sell many of these?"

"It goes in spurts. After Craig Grasmeyer's death, we sold a bunch. The sales have dropped off now that his killer is behind bars," Charlotte said. "Thanks, in part, to you."

"Yes, quite by accident, though," Jo said. "Do you keep records of how many and when these were sold?"

"Yes, for inventory purposes." Charlotte frowned. "Is there something specific you want to know?"

"Maybe. Could you tell me when you last sold one of these?"

"Sure."

Jo snapped a quick picture of the lock with her cell phone's camera before returning it to the rack. The trio returned to the back, and Charlotte stepped behind the counter. "It will take me a minute to pull up the records."

"Take your time." Jo leaned an elbow on the counter, her eyes scanning the shelves. "You have a little of everything in here."

"It is a hodgepodge of stuff. I'm becoming a hoarder, always looking for new and interesting things to sell," Charlotte confessed.

"I'm the same way. The mercantile is my catchall for whatever catches my fancy. It's easy to do."

"Yes, it is." Charlotte tapped the keys and then reached for the mouse. "The deadbolt you were asking about. Yes, we sold one two days ago. It's one of the pricier brands we carry. Before that, it was a few weeks ago, right after Grasmeyer's death."

"So you sold the lock two days ago. Any idea who you sold it to?"

Charlotte slowly shook her head. "No. There's no way to check on the inventory screen. I would have to sort through all of the receipts for that day."

"I don't want you to have to go to all that trouble," Jo said. "What you've told me is helpful."

Charlotte followed Raylene and Jo to the front entrance. "I need to stop by your bakeshop soon. Wayne has been bugging me to get over there and buy a batch of Delta's coconut macaroons."

"Delta makes those on Mondays," Raylene said. "They are delicious."

Jo thanked Charlotte for the information, and the women exited the store. "If you don't mind, I would like to stop by the deli for a quick chat with Marlee."

"Of course I don't mind," Raylene said.

The women crossed the street and stepped inside the deli. Marlee was in the front, talking to a diner. She caught Jo's eye as they passed by on their way to the back, and then joined them near the server station moments later. "I'm surprised to see you again."

"I stopped by Wayne's hardware store." Jo turned her cell phone on and clicked on the picture she'd taken of the door lock. "Do you recognize this?"

Marlee studied the picture. "No."

"It looks like the one we saw at Mary's place."

"I. Yes, now that you mention it, it does look like the lock that was on Mary's front door."

"It was a new lock," Jo said.

"Yes. In fact, Mary said she'd just installed it."

"Mary *purchased* the lock the day before Ashley went missing."

Marlee handed her the phone. "Are you sure?"

"Not a hundred percent." Jo slipped the phone inside her purse. "Charlotte, over at the hardware store, looked it up. A lock identical to the one on Mary's front door was sold two days ago, the day before Ashley went missing."

Raylene spoke. "You think Mary knew someone was going to bust down her front door and bought a lock before it happened?"

"I think there's a chance Mary and Ashley staged Ashley's disappearance." Jo quickly continued. "Think about it. Ashley is in deep doo. Her partner in crime is dead, there's another suspect still out there on the loose, possibly Janet's killer. She's being investigated. She needed to disappear, and she needed someone to help her do it."

"So her mother helped her." Marlee shook her head. "Maybe Ashley is trying to get her hands on the tickets and cash we found in my upstairs storage closet."

Jo rubbed the palms of her hands together. "I thought the tickets were placed inside the closet after Janet's death, but what if they weren't? What if it was Ashley and Janet's last big-ticket theft? What if the tickets had been delivered, but not yet put out for sale?"

Raylene picked up. "Ashley put Janet in charge of the tickets safekeeping; she placed them in a plastic bag in the storage closet, certain no one would find them."

"Other than me, she was the only other person who went up there," Marlee said.

"She could have made a copy of the upstairs key," Jo pointed out. "Ashley knows there's another stash of tickets somewhere here at the deli. She's the one who's been snooping around, trying to find them."

"Which means there's a good chance there wasn't a third party involved. It was always only Ashley and Janet." Jo began to pace. "Ashley or the culprit will come here again to track down the tickets and cash. If Mary, Ashley's mother is involved, she could possibly lead us to her."

"We can't be in two places at once," Marlee said. "Besides, I'm waiting on Detective Zylstra, the detective filling in, to get here. He's should be here within the hour."

Jo glanced at her watch. "Time is running out."

"I'm up for a little surveillance," Raylene said.

"I am, too," Jo said. "First, we need to swing by the farm to grab a couple of things and then drive out to Ashley and Mary's place."

Chapter 24

After a couple of wrong turns and having to backtrack, Jo finally remembered how to get to Mary and Ashley's single wide mobile home. She pointed to it as they drove past. "That's it."

"Now we need to find a place to park." Raylene peered out the windshield. "Drive to the next intersection and turn around."

"You're the expert." Jo drove to the intersection and then turned around. "We could park over there." She motioned toward a ramshackle corncrib leaning to the left as if a good, strong wind would easily topple it.

"Nope. It's too exposed."

"True." Jo studied the surroundings. "Their place is in the wide open."

"That might work." Raylene pointed to a cluster of trees lining the edge of the field one road over.

They drove past the mobile home a second time and Jo turned onto the dirt road. She eased off the gas as the vehicle bounced along the rutted road.

"Good grief." Raylene massaged her temples.

"This might not work." Jo shot her passenger a worried look. "We don't need to have your headache coming back."

She steered the vehicle off the side of the road, near the edge of the tree line and shifted into park.

"We can still see their place from here. What if someone comes along and asks what we're doing?"

"No worries. This is surveillance 101." Raylene swung the passenger door open. "We have options. We can go with an explanation your engine is overheating, which isn't entirely believable in a newer, high-end SUV or one which would be more believable."

"We ran out of gas," Jo guessed.

"Yep."

"So now what…oh great bounty hunter," Jo teased.

"We wait and watch." Raylene reached into the backseat, grabbed two sets of binoculars and handed one to Jo. "We'll want to stay close to the vehicle in case we need to make a fast move and pursue our target."

"Right." Jo tentatively stepped out of the vehicle, keeping one eye on the tall weeds rustling near her feet. She jerked her foot back. "On second thought, I'll stay here."

Raylene leaned both elbows on the hood of the SUV and adjusted the binoculars. She stayed in the same position for a long time before taking a break. She lifted both hands over her head in a long stretch.

Jo wrinkled her nose. "This is boring."

"It can be."

"What did you like best about being a bounty hunter?"

"Catching the bad guys and collecting our money." Raylene cleared her throat. "I have a confession to make."

Jo could tell by the tone of her voice that it was something serious. "Okay," she replied evenly.

"The first day we met, when Pastor Murphy brought me to the farm, I didn't lie when I told you I had nowhere to go, no family." She lowered her gaze. "No one cared until I met you and Delta and the other women."

Raylene opened her mouth and then promptly shut it; her eyes searching Jo's face as if seeking some sort of confirmation.

"We do care, Raylene. We all care very much. You're a part of the family. Even after you move on, we're still family."

"I feel the same."

"So that's your confession?"

"No. I...I have money." She hurried on. "I socked most of the money I made from being a bounty hunter in an account. It's in Florida. I haven't touched it."

"I see." Jo shifted the binoculars. "You have money."

"In the beginning, I wasn't going to stay at *Second Chance,* so it didn't matter. After I found out I was staying, I kind of put off telling you about the money because I thought you would make me leave."

"Why would I make you leave?"

"Because I could take care of myself."

Jo scratched the side of her forehead. "Perhaps you were financially prepared to leave prison, but what about emotionally?"

"I was a wreck, which is why I jumped off *Divine Bridge.*"

"So you weren't prepared to be out on your own," Jo said. "Money will only get you so far. There are other things equally as important. I've been down that road."

Raylene kicked at the pebbles on the ground. "I was wondering, you know, the money is just sitting in the bank, I can pay for my keep at the farm."

Jo, touched by Raylene's offer, blinked back sudden tears. "That is a thoughtful offer, Raylene, and it means more to me than you can possibly imagine. I want you to hang onto your money. You'll need it someday."

"Are you sure?"

"Positive."

"I had plans, big plans. Brock and I...we were going to expand our business. We were going to be big-time bounty hunters." Raylene laughed bitterly.

"All of those plans changed in the blink of an eye. Just like that." She snapped her fingers.

"No one is promised even one moment. Only God knows how many days each of us has."

"Believe me I realize that now."

"Thank you so much for telling me your secret...or what you thought was a secret," Jo said. "I appreciate the offer but the farm is self-sufficient, and I have enough money of my own to cover expenses if need be."

"If you change your mind, let me know," Raylene said.

"I will." Jo smiled softly, silently thanking God for moments like this. She started to say something else when Raylene's hand shot up. "We got a live one."

She shoved the binoculars to her eyes. "Middle-aged woman, heavy-set, hurrying to a red Honda parked in the drive. She's getting in. She's on the move!"

Raylene darted to the passenger side and hopped in.

Jo started the vehicle and shifted into drive. The tires spun, tossing a spray of gravel behind them as she veered onto the road. She kept as close to the edge of the road and as far away from the ruts as possible.

Despite traveling at a quick speed, the Honda and Mary Edison were gone by the time they reached the corner.

"Turn right," Raylene said.

With a quick glance to check for oncoming traffic, Jo careened onto the road and hit the gas. The SUV sped along at a fast clip.

They caught up with the vehicle two stop signs ahead and then Jo slowed, following behind at a distance.

When they reached town, the Honda turned right and away from Main Street.

Jo continued to maintain a safe distance yet close enough to keep a visual on the Honda. They circled the block and headed back toward town; Jo became suspicious Mary knew she was being followed. "She's onto us."

"When we get to town, turn in a different direction."

They passed *Four Corners Mini-Mart*. The Honda turned onto Main Street. Jo kept going. "Now what?"

"We catch up with her at the other end of town...hopefully."

Jo did as Raylene suggested, and they took several back streets running parallel to Main Street until they reached the end. The red Honda was nowhere in sight.

Jo sighed. "That was a waste of time. We lost Mary."

"Maybe." Raylene consulted the rearview mirror. "Let's hang out here until someone comes up behind us and forces us to move."

They sat there for several long moments until a pickup truck pulled up behind them. "We gotta keep moving. It looks like Mary went in a different direction. Let's head back to Marlee's place to check on her."

Jo turned right toward Main Street.

"Check it out." Raylene pointed to a vehicle heading in the opposite direction. It was the now-familiar Honda. "Did you see that?"

"Yes. It was the red Honda," Jo said.

"I could've sworn I saw a second person seated in the passenger seat."

"Are you sure?"

"I'm almost positive, but almost like they were ducking down or something. We need to follow them."

Jo eyed her rearview mirror, noting the Honda had reached the end of the main road. "Mary is turning back toward her place."

"We need to follow her. Jo!"

Jo looked away for only a fraction of a second, yet long enough for her to miss the fact that the car ahead of her had suddenly stopped.

The women flew forward on impact. Thankfully, the seatbelts caught them, and they whiplashed back. "Oh my gosh."

The car ahead of them pulled off to the side and Jo followed behind. She sprang from the vehicle and hurried to the driver's side. "I'm so sorry. I didn't see you stop to make a turn."

The man behind the wheel unbuckled his seatbelt. He exited the car and walked to the back. There was a small mark on the man's bumper. Jo wasn't quite as lucky. There was a larger scratch on the front bumper of the SUV.

"It's just a small scuff." The man rubbed his finger across the mark. "It'll cost me more to pay my deductible than to have someone fix it."

"This was my fault. I'll pay for the repair." Jo and the man exchanged contact information before returning to their vehicles. She waited until he drove off. "His bumper has a tiny scratch. Mine is slightly larger."

"Is he going to file a claim?"

"No. I told him to send me the bill for the repair." Jo consulted her side mirror before cautiously pulling back onto the street. "Thank goodness we weren't going very fast."

"It's my fault. I'm sorry for distracting you," Raylene apologized.

"No, it's my fault for not paying attention." Jo was much more cautious as she drove to *Divine Delicatessen*. She pulled in next to what she suspected was an unmarked police vehicle. "It looks as if the detective or his replacement finally showed up. I'll send Marlee a text."

Jo tapped out a quick message. "We're already in town. It won't hurt to take another drive by Mary and Ashley's place to see if we can see anything."

Instead of turning toward home, Jo drove back to the mobile home. "We need to make sure we don't draw attention to ourselves. I think Mary is already suspicious."

"I say we park on the side road again. We can hoof it through the farm field and come up along the back side of the mobile home," Raylene said.

"What if we get caught?"

"We're not going to get caught. Mary isn't going to go wandering around behind her place. If Ashley was in the car with her mother, she's hiding. She definitely won't be wandering around in plain sight."

"But what about you?" Jo asked. "If Mary reports you for trespassing, there's a chance you could get in trouble."

"A slim chance," Raylene said. "Besides, I'm the professional, and I don't plan on getting caught."

During the ride back to the mobile home, Raylene and Jo discussed Mary's trip to town. "What's interesting to me is I remember someone telling me that Mary didn't drive."

"Well, she was driving today," Raylene said. "I think she drove into town, picked someone up and then drove back home."

"This is pure speculation. We could be way off."

"Which is why a stop back by their place is worth the risk." Raylene sucked in a breath. "I have a theory."

"I'm all ears."

"Janet and Ashley were partners in the lottery ticket scheme. They had some sort of falling out after the mini-mart's manager became suspicious of the missing tickets. Janet freaked out. She went on a rampage inside the mini-mart and then stormed out. Ashley followed her back to the deli. They argued in the parking lot behind the deli, and that's when Ashley strangled Janet."

"I'm following. It's plausible so far."

"It could be that the morning of her death, Ashley and Janet pulled off another big-ticket theft. You mentioned the tickets were new, so the tickets had to have been stolen near the time of her death. Janet had a key to the deli's upstairs. She hid the bag in the closet after returning to the deli and planned to go back for them after her shift ended."

"She finished hiding the tickets. After hiding the tickets, she was confronted by her killer - possibly Ashley," Jo said. "That makes sense."

"And then we have Ashley," Raylene said. "With the heat on her, she was desperate to do something, so she staged her own kidnapping."

"With the help of her mother," Jo said.

"Yes. She's in hiding and still looking for the tickets and cash."

"Unless it's another employee," Jo said. "Remember the notebook."

They returned to their previous stakeout spot, and Jo pulled onto the side of the dirt road.

Raylene motioned toward the back of the trailer. "Do they have a dog, an animal that might alert them to someone near the property?"

Jo thought about it for a moment. "Nope. No pets that I noticed during our visit. Are we sure we want to do this?"

Raylene answered Jo's question with one of her own. "Do you want to find out if Ashley is alive and hiding?"

"Yes."

The women met near the front of the vehicle. An overwhelming feeling of impending doom filled Jo. "I hope we're not making a mistake."

"Would you rather wait here?" Raylene asked.

"No. I don't want you to have to go it alone since I was the one who dragged you into this mess."

"Sherry is my friend, my best friend. I want to clear her name as much as you do."

"Right. I guess I have my answer. Let's go."

The women hunched forward, creeping toward the back of the mobile home. They stayed close to the tree line until they were parallel with the place.

Raylene dropped to her knees. She pulled the binoculars from the case and adjusted the dial as she trained them on the home. "The red Honda is parked close to the deck and front door."

"Meaning Mary parked close to possibly ensure her passenger was able to get inside quickly."

"Correct," Raylene said. "The lights are on - a good sign someone is inside." Her eyes scanned the length of the mobile home. "I see movement. We're still too far away for me to get a clear visual. We'll have to move in closer."

Jo lifted her gaze to the darkening skies. "We can't just walk across the field. Someone might spot us."

"We'll have to wait it out until we can proceed after it gets dark."

"I better give Delta a heads up to let her know we won't be home for dinner." Jo tugged her cell phone from her pocket and tapped out a message. "Hopefully, she'll save us some leftovers. I'm starving."

"Me, too. It won't be long. Keep your phone handy. We may want to snap a couple of pictures."

Jo shifted several times, from sitting to kneeling and then finally standing as her back threatened to spasm and her calf muscles groaned in protest. She massaged her back as she began walking in circles.

Raylene shot her a quick look. "You okay?"

"Yes. Just having some twitches and tingles. It comes with old age."

"Right," Raylene snorted. "You're in better shape than me."

"I doubt that."

"I think it's safe to start moving again." Raylene and Jo slowly trekked toward the back of the mobile home.

Every few feet, Raylene motioned to Jo to stop as she surveyed their surroundings. It was a slow and tedious trip. Finally, they cleared the fields and reached the edge of the yard. "Over there."

The women tiptoed to a storage shed and eased in behind it. Raylene peeked around the corner. "I have a visual. Looks like the kitchen window.

There's an older woman, gray hair, late fifties, stocky, the same one I saw earlier."

"That's Mary," Jo said.

"She's talking to someone, but I can't see who it is. She stepped away from the window."

"What's that?" A bright light bounced off the front of the storage shed.

"It's a car." Raylene pressed on Jo's back, forcing her to the ground before falling face down next to her. "Don't move."

Bright beams of light bounced off the side of the shed, mere feet from where the women were hiding. Jo squeezed her eyes shut; praying whoever it was wouldn't see them.

The lights went out, and then a car door slammed. She could hear a muffled male voice and then a female voice coming from the front of the mobile home before fading as they walked to the other side.

Jo lifted her head. "Were you able to see anything?"

"With me kissing the ground? No. It was a male voice and then I heard a female voice."

"What about the vehicle?" Jo whispered.

Raylene handed Jo the binoculars. "Stay here. I'm going to try to get closer." She slithered forward on her belly, carefully inching her way toward the edge of the wooden deck.

Jo prayed Raylene wouldn't be seen. The feeling of impending doom returned with a vengeance. Something wasn't right. What if the women had stepped...or crept into some sort of a trap?

She thought about calling for Raylene to come back, but she was too far away.

Raylene made it to the end of the deck before adjusting her position. There was a loud banging sound and more voices as the man and woman came back into view and made their way to the deck steps.

Get down! Jo's mind screamed to Raylene.

Raylene curled into a ball and rolled under the deck.

Jo watched in horror as the silhouette of a man and the outline of Mary stepped closer to Raylene's hiding spot. They stood talking for several moments before the man returned to his car. She could hear him yell something before he climbed inside and drove off, his tires squealing.

Mary stood watching until he pulled out of the driveway and the vehicle disappeared from sight. The woman didn't move for several long moments.

Jo squeezed her eyes shut; all the while praying she wouldn't spot Raylene. *Please, Mary. Go back inside.*

Finally, the woman slowly turned and made her way inside. The door slammed, and Jo let out the breath she'd been holding.

Raylene crawled out from under the deck and then scrambled across the lawn to Jo's hiding spot.

"I thought we were goners."

"It was a close call." Raylene dusted off her hands.

"Were you able to take a closer look at the vehicle?"

"No. My window of opportunity went out the window when they walked back around to the other side of the deck."

"This was a total waste of time."

"It wasn't. We need to get out of here and head back to Marlee's. She may get some unexpected after hours company at the deli again tonight."

"Ashley and her mom?"

"Nope."

*****

Under the cover of darkness, the women began making their way back to the SUV. Jo made a slower trek as she navigated the uneven terrain, anxious to avoid critters that ventured out after dark.

Raylene slowed to keep pace with Jo. Neither of them spoke until they were safely inside the vehicle and the doors were locked. "Who was that?"

"I don't know. It was a male voice, but I didn't hear a name."

"What did he say?"

"He was yelling. I couldn't hear everything, but he said something about knowing Ashley was hiding, he was still looking for the tickets and he told Mary he'd be back."

"What did Mary say?" Jo asked.

"She swore she didn't know where Ashley was, and she told him if he didn't leave, she was going to call the cops."

Jo circled Main Street before pulling into an empty spot. The deli had just closed, but the lights were on. The women exited the vehicle and approached the window. She caught a glimpse of Marlee sweeping under one of the tables.

"Marlee." Jo tapped lightly on the front window.

Marlee lifted her head. She gave Jo a small wave before propping the broom against the wall and hurrying to the door. "Did you get my message?"

"No." Jo shook her head. "We were over at Mary's house, doing a little intel."

"You shouldn't have bothered. There's a detective in the back and a few more on the way. I have a confession." Marlee glanced over her shoulder and lowered her voice. "I wasn't supposed to say anything, but the investigators set up a sting last night, and they're setting up a second sting tonight to hopefully catch the culprit and possibly Janet's killer."

"Then you might want to mention to them that a man stopped by Mary and Ashley's place a short time ago. Raylene overheard him talking about Ashley and the tickets," Jo said.

"From what I could tell, this man and/or Ashley may have been here searching for the tickets and cash," Raylene said.

"Owen," Jo's eyes widened. "Maybe it was Owen Cole, Janet's boyfriend, you overheard. Think about it...chances are he knew about the lottery scheme."

"You think Owen killed Janet?" Marlee's jaw dropped.

"It's a possibility. It could have been Owen, Ashley or even Ashley's mother."

"But why kill Janet?" Marlee asked. "The woman was already in trouble."

"We'll find out, hopefully soon," Jo said. "We followed Mary in Ashley's car. We think she picked someone up - maybe Ashley - and took her back home."

"She's there now?"

"I think so, although I didn't see anyone other than Mary and the man who showed up," Raylene said.

Marlee jabbed her finger toward the back of the deli. "I'm going to give the detective a heads up. You may have some explaining to do later."

"I'm sure," Jo sighed. "It won't be the first time. We need to try to leave Raylene out of it because of her history."

"I will." Marlee followed them to the sidewalk. "I'm on my way out, too."

"It's almost over. Soon, life will return to normal," Jo said.

"Whatever that is."

"I'm ready to head home," Raylene said. "About those Advil? I think I'm going to need a couple more."

Chapter 25

Delta was waiting by the door when Raylene and Jo arrived back at the farm. "I was getting worried about you. What have you two been up to?"

"A little surveillance." Jo hung the keys on the hook and patted her stomach. "I'm starving."

"Me, too," Raylene said.

"Lucky for you, I saved some leftovers." Delta pulled two plates from the fridge. "It'll only take a couple of minutes to warm the food. So where were you?"

"At Mary and Ashley Edison's place," Jo said. "We believe Ashley is in hiding, thanks to her mother."

"She's on the lam because the heat is on," Delta said.

"I like your lingo," Raylene teased.

"I've watched me a crime show or two. Do you think Ashley killed Janet?"

"We're not sure. There's a third party involved - a male," Jo said. "It may have been Janet's boyfriend, Owen."

Jo continued. "While we were snooping around Mary's place to see if we could get a visual on Ashley, a man showed up. Raylene overheard him talking to Mary. He told her that he knew Ashley was in hiding, and he was still trying to get his hands on the tickets. I'm sure he wants the cash, too."

"You couldn't see who it was?"

"It was too dark," Raylene said.

"Good gravy." The microwave beeped, and Delta pulled the plate out before setting the second plate inside. "Maybe they were all in cahoots - Mary, Ashley, the man…"

"The investigators set up a sting at the deli, and Marlee promised to call us as soon as she knows something," Jo said.

The subject drifted to the activities around the farm. "We were going to put the fall decorations up after dinner," Delta reminded Jo.

"I...I'm sorry, Delta. I completely forgot."

"We'll do it tomorrow instead. The women were fine with waiting. Nash has been up here a couple of times since dinner." Delta set the plates of food on the table. "I think he's worried about you."

"For good reason." Raylene grabbed two forks from the silverware drawer and handed one to Jo.

Jo sent Nash a quick text, telling him she was home if he needed her. "I sent him a text." She gobbled her food but noticed Raylene was eating much slower. "Are you feeling all right?"

"My headache is threatening to return."

"I'll get you more pain relievers." Jo hopped out of the chair and headed to the locked medicine chest. She handed Raylene two tablets. "These are for later. I'm sorry for dragging you along tonight."

"Thanks." Raylene slipped them into her pocket. "Don't blame yourself. I wanted to come along, to try to help clear Sherry's name."

"I know, but you didn't know what you were getting yourself into."

"Yes...yes, I did. Besides, I call tonight's surveillance mission a success."

"Me, too." They finished their food and Jo insisted Raylene head back to her apartment to rest.

After she left, Jo washed their dishes while Delta dried.

"You hear anything yet from Miles Parker?" Delta asked.

"Nope. Not a peep. It's stressful waiting to see if...or when he moves forward with his claim."

"We just gotta keep praying about it." Delta retired before Jo, who plunked down on the living room couch and began mindlessly flipping through the channels.

She finally gave up on Marlee's call and checked to make sure the house was locked before Duke and she headed upstairs. She quickly brushed her teeth and washed her face before changing into her pajamas and crawling into bed.

Despite the adrenaline rush and the evening's adventure, Jo promptly fell asleep. She slept through the night and woke early. The first thing she did was check her cell phone, but there was no missed call from Marlee.

She hurriedly dressed and headed downstairs where she found Marlee and Delta in the kitchen. "Marlee. What are you doing here?"

"Hi, Jo. I'm sorry I didn't call last night. It was late, and I figured you would be asleep. Besides, I wanted to tell you in person what happened."

"Have you been waiting long?" Jo grabbed the coffee pot. She refilled Delta and Marlee's cups before pouring a cup for herself.

"No. I just got here." Marlee dumped a dash of creamer in her coffee cup. "You'll never guess who showed up."

"Owen."

"Nope. Carlos."

Jo lifted a brow. "Your Carlos?"

"Yes, my Carlos. I can't believe it. I'm still in shock. Turns out, Ashley and Carlos were an item, and he was also involved in the lottery scheme. The authorities caught him red-handed with the bag of goods after he broke in upstairs. He confessed before they even got him to the station."

Marlee continued. "Carlos told the authorities that Ashley and Janet got into an argument the day she quit the mini-mart. Janet stormed out with the tickets and cash. As soon as Janet left, Ashley called him to tell him what happened and that she thought

Janet was on her way back to the deli. Carlos planned to confront Janet as soon as she returned to work. When she didn't show up, he went looking for her and found her in her car. He told her he knew about the tickets and cash. He demanded that she hand them over but she refused. They argued in her car, he strangled her and returned to work as if nothing had happened."

"What about Ashley?" Jo asked.

"You were right. She was hiding out at home. When I told the investigators what you said, they drove to Mary and Ashley's home and found her there," Marlee said. "Ashley confessed to the ticket scheme and to arguing with Janet. When she found out about Janet's murder, she freaked out and suspected Carlos had killed her, so she went into hiding. She faked her own kidnapping with the help of her mother."

"Why didn't Ashley just go to the police?" Delta asked.

"She said after arguing with Janet and being under investigation for the ticket scheme, she was afraid that the authorities would pin the murder on her."

"That makes sense," Jo said thoughtfully. "The mini-mart manager was already looking into the missing tickets. It was only a matter of time before they figured out that Janet and Ashley were involved. Ashley and her mother were hoping she could hide out until the authorities captured Janet's killer - Carlos."

"What about the notebook?" Delta asked.

"The authorities believe Janet must have suspected someone else was involved in the scheme and was keeping notes. She apparently never suspected it was Carlos."

"So Carlos was the one trying to pry the employee lockers open. Wow." Jo blew air through thinned lips. "Ashley could well have been convicted of not only the scheme to defraud but also Janet's murder."

"And no one would have been the wiser. Which means I'm in the market for a new cook, not to mention a couple of extra servers. Speaking of cooks..." Marlee eyed Delta over the rim of her cup. "Are you still planning on entering the fall festival's baking contest?"

"It depends on who's asking...Marlee my friend or Marlee the competitor?"

Marlee chuckled. "A little of both."

"Well, then the answer is maybe," Delta answered evasively.

"You know I love you, Delta," Marlee teased.

"I love you too, Marlee, and that's why I'm not gonna give you an answer, but if I do." Delta lifted her coffee cup. "Here's to the best woman winning."

"Here. Here." Jo lifted her cup in a toast. "Here's to *two* of the best women winning."

The end.

If you enjoyed reading "Divine Blindside," would you please take a moment to leave a review? It would mean so much to me. Thank you! Hope Callaghan

The series continues... Book 4 in the Divine Cozy Mystery series coming soon!

Books in This Series
Divine Cozy Mystery Series

Get Free eBooks and More

Sign up for my Free Cozy Mysteries Newsletter to get free and discounted ebooks, giveaways & soon-to-be-released books!

https://hopecallaghan.com/newsletter

Meet the Author

Hope loves to connect with her readers! Connect with her today!

Never miss another book deal! From your mobile phone, Text the word Books to 33222

Visit **hopecallaghan.com/newsletter** for special offers, free ebooks, & new releases!

Follow Hope:

Facebook:www.facebook.com/authorhopecallaghan

Amazon :www.amazon.com/Hope-Callaghan/e/B00OJ5X702

Pinterest:https://www.pinterest.com/cozymysteriesauthor

Hope Callaghan is an American author who loves to write Christian books, especially Christian Mystery and Cozy Mystery books. She has written more than 50 mystery books (and counting) in six series.

In March 2017, Hope won a Mom's Choice Award for her book, "Key to Savannah," Book 1 in the Made in Savannah Cozy Mystery Series.

Born and raised in a small town in West Michigan, she now lives in Florida with her husband.

She is the proud mother of one daughter and a stepdaughter and stepson. When she's not doing the thing she loves best - writing books - she enjoys cooking, traveling and reading books.

Raspberry Dream Bars Recipe

Ingredients:

#1 Crust:

2 cups crushed vanilla wafers

1 tablespoon white sugar

1/3 cup pecans, chopped

½ cup melted butter

#2 Center:

12 oz. whipped cream cheese

¾ cup powdered sugar

1 cup seedless raspberry jam

#3 Topping:

3/4 cup brown sugar

1/2 cup all-purpose flour

1/2 cup oats

¾ teaspoon ground cinnamon

¾ teaspoon ground nutmeg

1/3 cup butter, melted

Directions:

-Preheat oven to 350 degrees.

-Grease bottom of 9x13 baking dish.

-Mix ingredients for crust: vanilla wafers, white sugar, pecans and melted butter.

-Press into bottom of greased baking dish.

-Mix/cream softened cream cheese and powdered sugar.

-Spread cream cheese mixture over top of the cookie crust.

-Whisk/cream raspberry jam with fork (makes it easier to spread)

-Spread seedless raspberry jam over top of cream cheese without touching edges of dish.

-Mix brown sugar, all-purpose flour, oats, cinnamon and nutmeg. Add melted butter.

-Sprinkle topping mixture over the raspberry spread.

-Bake in 350 degree preheated oven for around 30 minutes or until topping is light golden brown.

Let cool completely before cutting the bars and serving.

Made in the USA
Columbia, SC
13 June 2020

11014851R00217